Shattered Part III

*To: Judith Rose
Thank you for supporting me!
Peace & Blessings,
A.A. Jewell*

Also by DD Jewell

Shattered Part I
The Story of Giselle

Shattered Part II
The Story of John

DD JEWELL

Shattered Part III

The Story of Fatima

Copyright © 2017 by DD Jewell.

All Rights Reserved.

ISBN: 978-1-387-52000-8

No part of this book may be reproduced or transmitted in any form or by any means, electronic or mechanical, including photocopying, recording, or by any information storage and retrieval system, without permission in writing from the copyright owner.

This is a work of fiction. Names, characters, and incidents either are the product of the author's imagination or are used factiously, and any resemblance to any actual persons, living or dead, or events is entirely coincidental.

Book Cover designed by Channing Parham

Author Photo by Gulley Images

Printed in the United States of America

ACKNOWLEDGMENTS

Wow, book three, I can't believe it!!! I would like to thank a couple of people for their continuous support and encouragement in my writing process.

To Nick, my husband, thanks for allowing me to see God sculpt your life.

Thanks, Rogers Jewell, you are my Dad and have always been my biggest fan. Thank you for reading my books and bringing such lively and emotive conversations and feedback about the stories and characters.

To my sons, Amir and Sharif, you bring out the absolute best in me. I love you two so much.

Prologue

Later that evening, we met John and Damali for dinner. I was a little nervous because it was going to be awkward seeing John with someone other than my best friend. However, Larry calmed my nerves, and I felt well prepared for meeting Damali. When I first saw them, I greeted them as if they were old friends. But deep inside, it was awkward seeing a woman my Larry used to be in love with dating the man to whom my best friend used to be engaged. Life was so full of ironies. John seemed a bit on edge as if he was expecting me to bring up Giselle, but that would have been crass and disrespectful to all parties involved. Since the beginning of our relationship, Larry has always had a way of bringing out the best in me. I knew I was a changed woman given that I could even tolerate meeting Damali. After Marc, my ex before Larry, I did not want to date any guy who had female friends. Not only were Larry and Damali friends, she was also the last woman he had sex with before committing his life to celibacy until marriage. Damali knew something about Larry that I did not know and would not until we wed.

However, with Larry, I had such peace and trust in him like no other man I had known. In comparison to Marc, Larry was a rock, and Marc a piece of broken glass. Larry and I were connected, and the center of our connection was Christ, and He made all of the difference in me and us as a whole. As the night progressed, Larry and Damali went to the restroom, leaving John and me alone for the first time.

"From what I hear, Damali is a great lady," I said, looking at him with a raised brow seeking affirmation.

"She definitely is," he said with reluctance.

"I know Giselle's version of what happened between you two, and I'm a grown woman, John. Grown enough to know there's her side, your side, and the truth," I said, putting him at ease.

"You are so right," he said, breathing with deep relief.

"If you and Giselle were meant to be, then you would be together. I just want everybody to be happy. I want everyone to experience the love I have with Larry. It's like God handmade him for me," I said, as Damali and Larry returned.

"What are y'all talking about? Fill me in on the juicy details," Larry said, with his deep southern drawl.

"I was just telling John how much loving you has changed my life," I said, kissing him.

"You changed my life, added pepper to my salt," Larry said, returning my kiss.

"Salt and Peppa here, and we're in effect," I jested, as everyone laughed.

Before we went our separate ways, John thanked me for staying neutral and wished me all the happiness in the world. Damali hugged me and told me she was overjoyed by Larry and me. She had such a profound authenticity about her that I hugged her back. Everything was so calm and perfect. Nonetheless, my phone's vibration brought a cloud to my sunshine.

Have you ever dreaded returning someone's phone call because you knew the conversation would devastate that person? As Larry and I drove to his house, my phone was in constant mayhem with text messages from Giselle, which read "R u done w/ dinner yet?" A part of me wished I hadn't told Giselle that I was having dinner with her ex-fiancé, but it was inevitable for us to discuss him as he was dating one of Larry's friends.

"So, Love, what are you going to do?" Larry asked, probably becoming annoyed by my phone's constant notifications.

"I don't know. I could just call her tomorrow morning," I said, trying to escape the onus.

"Why put it off? You already know she's going to probe you about Damali," he said, with confidence.

"That's the problem. I don't have anything to say that she would want to hear," I replied, staring out the window hopelessly.

"There's not much to tell besides how Damali looks," he offered when I cut him off.

"We're talking about women here and a Black woman at that. She's gonna want to know not only if Damali looked good, but if she looks better than she does. She will want to know how John was acting, how they looked together, was Damali a bitch, and so on," I said, trying to give him a glimpse of what I had on my hands.

"You are known for being the straight shooter from the hip. This should be right up your alley," he said, smiling and kissing my hand.

"You are really getting a kick out of this, huh?" I asked already knowing the answer. Then my phone rang again. Larry looked at me, and I finally answered.

"Hey, Gee!" I exclaimed as if everything was normal.

"I have been blowing your phone up...," she began, but I quickly interrupted.

"I know, we haven't too long finished dinner," I replied.

"So?" she insisted.

"John's doing well, and Damali is a nice person," I answered, trying to cut to the chase.

"And?" she hissed.

"And they seem happy?" I replied, trying to think of what else she would like to know.

"Did he ask about me? Well, never mind. That would have been rude with her around," she both asked and replied.

"To be quite frank, John and I had time alone. So, to answer your question, no he didn't mention you. I brought up the elephant in the room and told him your relationship had two sides, and I wish the best for both of you," I said finally getting it out.

"What do you mean two sides? I am your best friend, and my side is the true side," she vented.

"Giselle, there are always three sides to every story, both person's, and the truth," I responded, slightly annoyed.

"Wow, excuse me. So, I guess Damali will be your maid of honor also," she continued, with offense dowsed with sarcasm.

"If you don't want to be in my wedding, let me know, but last time I checked, you were my maid of honor," I said, as my thermostat began to rise.

"I am sorry! I just don't know how to feel about all of this. I don't remember how she looks from that one time I ran into her at John's apartment. Do you think she's pretty?" she asked, changing topics like the weather.

"She's beautiful, both inside and out. You will eventually meet her," I said, forewarning her.

"I guess I need to prepare myself for that," she said in a low voice as if she was holding back tears.

"Giselle, I wish I could tell you that Damali was horrible and John seemed miserable without you, but that is just not the case."

"For Pete's sake, I see why Larry, John, and any man would love her. She is Damali. She's authentic, caring, smart, generous, and Christ-centered," I said, forgetting Larry was in the car with me.

"Wow, she sounds perfect! Well maybe he needs someone like Mother Teresa," she rebutted. "I don't walk on water, part the seas, or feed the hungry. I just try to be the best me I can be. If that's not good enough, then I don't know what is."

"Giselle, it is over! You and John are over! Damali did not break you two up! You need to get a grip! Sometimes you like seeing yourself as the victim! But in this instance, you're a woman who has a failed relationship. Join the damn club and keep it moving!"

I finally unleashed the beast. Giselle has always had a tendency to be stuck on herself to a fault. I figured that was the main reason why her relationship with John failed twice.

"How dare you judge me in my vulnerability, Fatima! Just because someone finally fell in love with you, you think you have the right to look down on others? I held your hand on more than one occasion while you were on a table...," she began, spewing venom before I cut her off.

"Giselle, before you finish your sentence, we need to get off this phone. I know where the fuck I have been, the times your hands were there and the times they weren't. I know who the fuck I was, and I know who I am now, and who I want to be. And yes, finally, I have a man who loves me. He knows the whos, whats, and whens and still chooses to love me, Fatima Antoinette Crosby! The unlikely candidate for a happy ending! I am not fucking judging anyone. I am living in my season, and fuck you and anybody else who can't be happy for me! So, before this turns uglier than what it already is, goodbye!" I said, hanging up on her still hot from the moment but regretting my reaction and words.

I couldn't look at Larry. I was livid, and I wanted to call her back and tell her some things about herself. Nonetheless, no good would come from that. The hardest part of becoming the new creation that Christ says we can be is the motherfucking past. It is like thorns, nails, and sometimes a spear in the side. I don't have doubts about who I can be when looking forward only when looking back. The reality of time is that no matter where you find yourself, you always have an audience who will never forget your actions. I am convinced the devil takes permanent *residence in our pasts, and God abides with us in the now. However, we are continually making each moment the past. The past is as real as yesterday. I am trying to make better decisions in my now so my yesterdays won't be painted with regret.*

1 | The Other Woman

The morning of my 25th birthday, I was home in southeast DC in my 2-bedroom brownstone finishing out winter break from grad school. Later that evening, I would drive back to Charlottesville, Virginia for a party I was having at my apartment with friends traveling both near and far. In the meantime, I had some business to finish before I got back to the books.

"Are you going to come over here before you go back?" my mother insisted.

"Yes mother, if I have time," I said, looking at the text message on my phone, which read, *otw*. I got horny in anticipation of seeing him.

"What are you doing now? Why can't you come now?" she asked on the verge of giving me a headache.

"I am cleaning, and I have some other things to take care of," I answered.

I didn't want to tell her the whole truth, so I gave her part of it. I was cleaning my bedroom earlier. I was refreshing my body before she called. The other things I had to do consisted of a 6'1" milk chocolate mound of muscles.

"Mom, I have to go. I'll call you later," I said, rushing off the phone because of the playful knock on my door.

"Happy birthday, baby," he said, in his raspy, baritone voice while grabbing me around the waist and lifting all 145 pounds of me off the floor with one hand. I loved how strong and sexy he was.

"Thank you," I said slowly penetrating his mouth with my tongue. Wet and ready is where I found myself with this man I had seen for a year to the exact date.

"I love your outfit," he said, examining my birthday suit.

Some men liked lingerie, some men liked chicks wearing their shit, some men liked the nude, and some men didn't give a damn as long as snatch was attached. Charles loved the nude. He also loved a full bush that was neatly trimmed. Some men liked chicks' Hello Kitties bald. Charles was also a butt-man, and that was one of my biggest assets.

"I have an appointment in an hour, and then I have to pick up little man," he said, referring to his 16-month old son.

"I understand," I said, sounding like a broken record for the umpteenth time.

"I am hungry," he said, placing me on the kitchen counter.

"Oh, are you?" I asked, knowing exactly what he was about to do.

Dr. Charles Chappelle, being an OB-GYN, knew my body too well as if he created it. Not only could he make me come in every way imaginable, but he also made me squirt. I thought "squirting" was a myth until I met him. He educated me and talked me through the whole thing as he pointed out the different areas of my vagina with his thick tongue. He told me areas of my vagina I didn't know existed like the Bartholin gland which played a major role in "squirting." The first time it happened I thought I had peed on myself, but I hadn't.

"This is so good," he said, licking and sucking.

All I could do is sigh and grab his head as he used his fingers like magic wands. As my glutes tensed when I climaxed, he placed me on the dining room table on my stomach. As he thrusted me, he continued to play with me. All I could do was moan and sigh; I thought I was going to pass out when I climaxed once again.

"Oh yeah baby, get that nut. I like it when you come on my dick," he said, releasing in me.

"Now, let's blow out the candles," he said, turning me back around and sucking me again while dousing his tongue with both of our secretions.

He was so nasty, and I loved every bit of it. With a wet face, he kissed me deeply as if he wanted to leave a piece of his soul inside of me.

"Mmm, don't you taste good?" he said with a soft, moist kiss on my forehead.

"I'm okay. You taste better," I said not meaning it at all.

Who gets pleasure out of tasting themselves and then the residuals of semen? Yuck! Being a woman, you learn how to ad-lib and fake some shit. Most men love fantasy more than reality. They want to believe they are the best chicks ever had. They want to believe women think they are sexy and that women live for the pure fact of sexing them. Yeah, okay.

Nevertheless, what I did not have to fake with Charles is the fact he was the best I had ever been with, and that's saying a lot. When I reached fifty sex partners, I stopped counting. Shit, I remember asking one of my best friends, Giselle, when we first became close how many men she had been with, and she said she was a virgin. We were both nineteen years old at that time. I felt like a slut because I had been with twenty guys at that time. It wasn't like my parents encouraged virginity or saving myself for marriage. When I got my period at twelve years old, they put me on the pill. There was no talk about sex outside of don't get pregnant.

"Damn, what does she want now?" Charles said, looking at her face before he answered his phone.

"Yes, love. I am picking him up from daycare. You're taking her to ballet, right? Ok, I will see you later. I love you too," he said, ending the call and grabbing my hand.

"I am sorry about that. She said she called the office and they said I was at lunch," he smirked.

"And indeed, that was the best lunch I have ever had," he said, kissing me on my forehead again.

"You don't think she knows? I think she knows," I sighed.

"And? I don't give a damn! She got the house of her dreams, the children she wanted, and tons of shit no one she knows will ever have," he spewed contempt and arrogance as he went to my bar to pour a dark rum on the rocks.

"Then why are you with her?" I insisted for the umpteenth time.

"When I was growing up, a man couldn't get an educated, street-smart, pretty, and sexy girl. If they possessed one of those qualities, they didn't possess the others. Educated usually meant dumb as a doorknob, lacking street savvy. Pretty meant a dud in the bed. Women like you didn't exist," he said, buttoning his pants.

"Well, that was then, and this is now. Why stay with a woman you are not in love with?" I insisted.

"I didn't marry for love; I married for a family. I stay married for the family. I believe that's why fate brought you to me so I could have something out of life. Have some of this thing called love," he said, winking at me.

"So, fate, huh? Well, what the fuck is fate giving me?" I said, becoming depressed.

"All of this," he said, grabbing his crouch and smiling.

"Great," I replied, looking at the floor.

"Look, baby, you know I love you. My heart belongs to you," he said, running to the door.

"Hold on one second while I go get a little glimpse of what fate has for you," he said, going to his car.

When he returned, he had four beautifully wrapped boxes.

"Oh my God! For me?" I asked.

"Today is not only your birthday but our one-year anniversary. One year ago, God sent me an angel. An angel to rescue my life," he said, kissing me.

"Here's just a small token of things to come in time. Baby, patience is all I am asking for," he said as he hugged me.

"How long Charles? Ten years? You are already ten years older than I am. Do I have to wait until you are old and gray, can't see, or walk?"

"Damn baby, 35 years old isn't all that old. I have many great years still ahead!"

"Well, I don't! Not before my eggs start turning into powder."

"You have at least another 15 years before you have any powder coming," he laughed.

"I am glad you find this funny," I said, trying to gather my feelings so my current situation wouldn't fuck up my day.

In the beautiful boxes were a Louis Vuitton handbag, two pairs of Christian Louboutin heels, and a David Yurman diamond cuff bracelet. There was a small note card in the bracelet's box which read: The other three gifts are your birthday presents, but this bracelet is for our anniversary. You are my heart, Fatima.

A man that drops nearly ten thousand dollars on you for your birthday must be in love. Well, at least it made me feel better thinking of it that way.

"Baby, look into my eyes," he said, grabbing my hands. "These are small tokens of how I feel about you. I love you," he said, kissing me softly on my lips.

"You know how to leave a girl speechless. Thank you, Charles, I love you too," I said, returning his kiss.

"Let's talk tomorrow so you can tell me all about your birthday party. Especially if any collegiate dudes try to hit on you," he said, trying to seem jealous.

"Don't worry about me. My bed will be empty tonight. What about yours?" I asked, winking at him as he left.

On my hour and a half drive back to Charlottesville, I couldn't help but remember a year ago when I met Charles. I stopped for gas on my way to a date when he pulled up next to me in a Jacquar XJL and insisted on pumping my gas. "Women shouldn't pump gas when men are around," he said, as he not only pumped my gas but paid for it. I was smitten by his good looks and charm. We exchanged numbers, and a couple of days later he asked me out for lunch. Without any signs of a wedding ring, I asked him if he was dating and he said no, getting off by the technicality of my question. I did not find out he was married until months into it. I took my time having sex with him because I was seeing a couple of other guys off and on, nothing serious. I told him I wouldn't have sex with him until I spent the night at his place. So, he took me to this beautiful condo in Montgomery County, MD. I checked the mail to see if his name was on it, and indeed, it read Dr. Charles Chappelle. There was no sign or hint of a woman.

I probably wouldn't have found out he was married for a long time because he was so good at living a double life. By the time he disclosed that he was married, we had been sexing like Jack Rabbits for a couple of months. When he told me his story, with tears in his eyes, it didn't sound cliché, but in retrospect, it is probably in the same book all married men who cheat read.

He married his college sweetheart that came from a good family. Nonetheless, he was not in love with her, but with the image that their life together presented to the world. They were two successful Black doctors who had two children (a boy and a girl), a million plus dollar home, and all the luxuries of life. He was active in his church and a hands-on father. He was an overall good guy minus the fact that he was an adulterer. He said he had only cheated on her once in their ten-year marriage, which was right after their daughter was born, five years after they wed. They were on the verge of divorcing, and he hooked up with a girl he had dated in high school. His wife, Simone, found out about it and they went through extensive couples counseling and decided to remain married.

When I met him, Charles Jr. was six months old, and they were on the verge of divorcing again. Charles said he was never in love with her, but loved their family. He promised me that he would not leave me hanging on forever; that he needed to end his marriage with the least amount of drama and some decency. He did not want me taking the blame for what was already broken. He didn't want me to be labeled the hoe that broke up the picture-perfect family because their marriage was a glass mosaic that was already falling apart.

Being the other woman was not my normal, and at times we went through some dark moments. When he thought he was losing me, he would make grand gestures like take me to Hawaii, which as far as Simone knew was a medical conference. He also had me come to their house when she left town to see her family. A couple of times, he brought little Charles to lunch with us. He also invited me to his daughter's first ballet recital. Although I could not sit with him, we saw each other, and I saw Simone live for the first time. She was pretty, but plain and probably a dud in the bed. Simone was dark skinned like him and much smaller than me, perhaps 115 pounds. She seemed to mask her unhappiness with a plastic smile. He appeared to be the doting husband and father. Later that night he came to my brownstone and sexed me like the end of the world was coming. When he got home later that evening, he posted a picture of him and his daughter and said one of the best days of my life, thanks life for showing me love. In the backdrop of their photo was me. I did not know I was captured in the picture until he Facebooked it.

When I told him, I was going back to school to get my MBA, he booked us a weekend in the Oriental Suite at the Mandarin Hotel in DC. We did the full day spa treatment and dinner at a restaurant in the hotel. We made love all night long until we parted ways. He returned to Simone after a "golf retreat" with his boys.

This past holiday season was our first and very depressing. I could not see him, and I was still grieving the loss of my father, Dr. Craig James Crosby, who died on Thanksgiving before my 24th birthday. Although my relationship with Charles was taboo, he was what I needed to help me grieve the loss of my father. The more happiness I felt with him the pain and resentment I felt thinking about my father subsided. In time, I started talking to other guys to ease the pain of being the *other woman*. However, I was expecting him to divorce and put a ring on it. If he didn't, then I wasn't going to waste my life bearing through someone else's shattered life. I deserved better, and I knew it.

2 | Options

I drove back to Charlottesville so I could celebrate the rest of my 25th birthday and begin my second semester of business school. I always knew I wanted to get a Master's degree, but once I started working and indulging in luxuries, it prolonged the journey back to school. Through unfortunate events, I found myself financially capable of returning to school. My father died the year prior, and he made sure our family was secure.

After my father's estate was settled, my parents' house in an exclusive gated golf community was paid off. My mother, Justine, began receiving annuity payments from his life insurance so that she could live comfortably until she died. Although her $200,000 yearly stipend should have been sufficient for her, she still supported my younger brother, Maurice. Maurice was four years my junior, and we were oil and vinegar. I have always been more hardcore, assertive, and independent while he was soft, passive, and needy. At times, I felt like I was more of a dude than he.

My brother and I were both left $500,000 a piece from our father that was dispersed in payments of a specific amount over time. My money was disbursed at a larger amount than Maurice because he had proven to be careless with money, especially when he dropped out of college to pursue a music career. However, with my money, I was able to go back to school full-time and maintain my bills, which were inconsequential especially since I owned my brownstone in southeast Washington, D.C. The brownstone was one of my father's properties that was paid off and willed to me. I owned my car, a 5 Series BMW, which was a graduation gift from my parents when I received my Bachelor's degree.

My journey back to school was met with elation when I discovered that my best friend and sands, Giselle "Gee" Gibson, was also returning. There were twenty-three Black students in the MBA program, but that made no difference to me because I was the quintessential networker. That was how I could live in a PHAT two-bedroom apartment off grounds with a white girl named Amanda, who I met during undergrad. She was a sweet, sheltered, southern girl who loved her family from some hick town not too far from Charlottesville. Most weekends, she was gone, which I was particularly glad the night of my birthday party.

Right before I came back to school, I met two guys, Marc and Jasper, at a club in DC. Jasper was from DC like I, and Marc, who was from Columbia, Maryland, was a 2nd-year Business grad student at my school. Although Marc was more handsome, Jasper had more swagger, charm, and conversation. I preferred assertive men over shy guys. After dating a couple of introverts, I learned that although they don't have much to say they have their fair share of drama, and most of it comes from low self-esteem and poor communication skills.

Jasper and I hit it off fast and starting sexing by the end of the week we met. I needed a diversion from Charles. I wasn't going to save myself for a married man. For all I knew, he was still sexing his wife. No man deserves to have such a feast. When I returned to school, Jasper said he would come and visit me especially since his best friend was a couple of miles up the road.

The weekend of my birthday, Jasper had been in town visiting Marc, and the two came to my birthday party. From the moment I saw them, I got a strange vibe that perhaps Marc was digging me too, but I didn't have the time to give it too much credence because I had a full plate: grad school, Charles, family drama, and match-making my best friend. I was trying to hook up Giselle with another 2nd-year student, John Anderson.

I hit on him during our 1st semester, but he dissed me. He seemed like a nice guy, and I wanted to see what it was like to try something different. He looked different, light-skinned with curly hair, and he acted differently, he wasn't a sex-crazed gawker. As fate would have it, it seemed I attracted dark-skinned womanizers. John appeared wholesome and asked me to introduce him to Giselle. Although it was a mild blow to my ego, I thought to myself *why the Hell not?* Somebody in life deserved happiness, so why not someone I loved.

My only true apprehension about them gelling was Giselle. Although she was my girl, she was a bit self-absorbed. She was a virgin, and because of that, she was an ice-woman. She took life too seriously for my liking. On the other hand, she might have thought the opposite of me. Sex was to me what drugs, alcohol, or food were to other people. It helped me cope with pain. Everyone has a vice whether known or unknown.

"Hello, John! It's about fucking time you got here, you pretty bastard," I said, hugging him with Giselle by my side.

"Well, I had a couple of things to take care of so I could stay a while and enjoy myself. Is that okay with you?" he asked, smiling probably happy to see Giselle by my side.

"John, honey, there is someone I want you to meet, my soror, friend, and confidant; the one that I have been telling you about, Giselle Gibson," I said, putting my arm around her shoulder.

She seemed tensed as hell. He extended his hand toward her.

"Giselle, this is John Anderson, the fine man who has Wall Street calling his pockets," I joked, breaking the tension.

"So, we finally meet. We have passed each other so many times. I feel as though I almost know you," he said, releasing her hand slowly.

"Yeah, I know," she smiled, like a little 5th-grade girl.

I wanted to kick her, but I was sure John would know how to handle her.

"Well, let me leave you two to mingle. As you see I have my hands full," I said, glancing at Jasper and Marc.

"About time," Jasper said, putting one hand around my waist. Men loved marking their territory.

The only problem was, we weren't exclusive, and I did not like public displays of affection with a boning partner. He knew this too, but I think he was intimidated by all the good-looking men there and not knowing who I had been intimate with was probably killing him.

"Hey Fatima, I like your playlist," Marc said, looking so delectable.

I think that was the first time I saw him smile at me.

"Wow, something Marc and I have in common! Go figure," I said while laughing and patting him on the back.

He smiled once again. I loved his smile.

"Yes, you two have a lot in common," Jasper remarked, piquing my interest.

"Like what?" I asked Jasper but hoping for Marc to answer.

"I heard you're a chef too," Marc replied, making me wonder how much Jasper had shared with him.

"So, you cook too?" I asked.

"I have a daughter so yes I know how to do a thing or two in the kitchen," he replied, giving me some info I didn't know.

"How old is your daughter?" I asked, becoming engulfed in our conversation as if Jasper wasn't there.

But as in true form, like any other Alpha Male, Jasper threw shade on Marc, disclosing personal baby-mama-drama. However, instead of responding to the information, I ignored it and diverted back to cooking.

"Did Jasper tell you I cooked for him or that I had some leftovers and he begged me for some?" I asked, throwing shade right back at him. I hated when people tried to make themselves look good by tearing someone else down.

"Oh, really?" Marc smirked.

The look on his face confirmed my suspicions that perhaps Jasper embellished a couple of things about me. One thing that I learned about best friends (both men and women), they usually share taste in the opposite sex. Sometimes they share a little too much information, in a grand form of bragging, and end up arousing their best friends' interests in their dates or significant others. I had been around that avenue a couple of times with "best friends."

For the rest of that evening, I divided myself among my guests, but no matter how engulfed I was in conversations my eyes could always find Marc. As the guests slowly exited, Jasper wanted badly to spend the night with me, but I declined. Charles had already satisfied my needs, and Jasper wasn't even close to Charles in the bed. Marc hugged me goodbye, which caught me off guard. That night, the extrovert and introvert became buddies.

Later that week when I saw him in passing, he offered his assistance in helping me in a class he overheard me complaining about at my party. I took him up on his offer although I knew we should not entertain too much time alone.

"Who is it?" I asked already knowing.

"Santa Claus," he jested as I opened the door only to behold a gorgeous man.

I was speechless.

"Is this how you dress and smell to tutor all the first-year girls?" I joked, trying to break the awkwardness I felt.

"Most of the time, I am bumming around campus looking collegiate, so from time to time, I like to wear my real clothes," he said, hugging me tighter than before.

I knew from that moment on Marc wanted to bone me, and I struggled with the thought of whether I should succumb.

"Well, you don't look too bad," I flirted, examining him head to toe and then turning my back quickly.

"Did you enjoy your party?" he asked, walking around observing my apartment.

"For the most part. Did you enjoy my party?" I asked while placing my books on the table hinting at studying.

"It was cool. I enjoyed talking to you. I feel like I know you a little better," he smiled.

"Really?" I asked, with my curiosity piqued.

"You seem like a nice girl. Why are you with Jasper? You need to protect yourself. All that glitters isn't gold. If you give too much of yourself too soon, you will get hurt. Guys like a challenge. That's what I tell all my female friends who come crying to me after some jerk has screwed over them," he said in a paternal tone.

"Wow, is that right? What are my intentions with Jasper, Dr. Phil?" I asked so he could pontificate further.

"From what I hear and what I have been shown, to be in a relationship," he answered.

"Is that what you know, think, or been led to believe? Don't answer. I am sexing Jasper and have no other plans for him. He is not relationship material and definitely not marriage material. He is a guy that gets off on eating me out, because he feels like he's so good at it. I talk shit with him because that's what guys like to hear," I answered him not caring whether he would tell Jasper but knowing that he wouldn't.

"Wow! I stand corrected. I thought…," he began, but I cut him off.

"Why are you doing so much thinking about me? Something Jasper shared with you captured your interest in poor naïve me?" I asked.

"I just thought you were a nice girl and…," he began again, but once again I interrupted him.

"And you thought by dropping dime on your simple ass small dick best friend that my pussy would become wet, and you could sample some too," I replied and laughed.

"Get out of here!" he responded, trying to seem wounded.

"You guys are alike," I said, shaking my head and looking into my notes.

"No, I'm actually one of the few good guys. I don't do half the shit dudes like Jasper do. I just chill," he said, grabbing my notes from my hand.

"So, you don't like sex? I know you aren't a virgin because you have a child," I said, finally getting up from the table and sitting down on the couch.

He followed me and sat almost on my lap.

"I don't get panties thrown at me like Jasper. If you haven't noticed, I am a shy guy," he said blushing.

"Yeah, but sexy as hell," I replied.

"So sexy that you met both of us at the same time, but picked him over me. That's the storyline of my life," he said, sounding pathetic.

"Please, save that shit for a reality TV show. You looked mean as hell and stuck up. You sent signals that you didn't want to be bothered."

"When we met, I had just gotten into a fight with Lynelle, my daughter's mother. Whatever I do concerning her is never good enough or to her standards."

"So, you do have baby mama drama. Jasper dropped a couple of dimes on you too," I laughed.

"Whatever! You think you are so smart," he said, gazing into my eyes.

"I am smart enough to know that you probably should leave right now because I am not going to get any work done," I said, trying to avoid a catastrophe.

"Oh, I am so sorry. Let's get started," he said, trying to buy time as I escorted him to the door.

"Let me make this up to you. You can come to my place and not only will I help you, but I'll also cook dinner for you," he offered.

"What will Jasper think of that?" I asked not caring. If he didn't care about his "best" friend, why should I?

"It's none of his business. You said it's not like that and he sure doesn't act like it either. Will you? Please!" he insisted.

I replied "yes" knowing that I was igniting a fire.

"Can you really cook? Because if not, we can go to a restaurant and Go Dutch?" I said, trying to avoid going to his place.

"Wow! Yes, I can cook, and I can also treat you to dinner. I may not come from a well-to-do family, but I'm not dirt poor," he said, seeming offended.

"Don't take it that way. I don't know what your financial situation is. I don't mind paying for my meal or even yours for that matter. And what do you mean by well-to-do family?" I inquired.

"It's no surprise Fatima; you come from money. I see your Red Bottoms, David Yurman jewelry, and your Gucci and Louis Vuitton purses. I'm surprised you would even give a guy like me time," he said, throwing me off guard.

"I like nice things, and a lot of what you see are gifts," I said, feeling uncomfortable being under his microscope.

"Are you used to getting what you want?" he asked.

"Material things, yes, for the most part. Other things, not so much," I replied, thinking of Charles.

"What are the other things?" he probed.

"Things that are out of my control. What about you? Are you used to getting what you want?" I deflected.

"Shoot, I don't know what that feels like. I have had to work hard for everything that I have. I am hoping that after graduation, when I start this job, I will finally be on top. Not as high on the mountain as you, but at least be at the foot of it," he said.

"Having money isn't all that," I began before he cut me off.

"Said no poor person. That's something rich people say, Fatima," he said as if he were setting the classism record straight.

"Marc, I was going to say money doesn't mean anything if you're not happy. My family is not rich, if so, I wouldn't be at the same business school as you. Now we may have more than some, but I am unapologetic about our socio-economic status. Is this going to be a problem for you?" I asked.

"No, I just don't want to disappoint you. Right now, I can't afford any of the things you are accustomed to. I thought I was going big buying my mother a Coach bag for Christmas. I came to b-school to make a better life for my daughter and me. I just don't want to waste your time," he replied.

"I have my own money and am not asking you for anything. I don't ask men for anything; my father equipped me so I wouldn't have to. Yes, I have dated some guys who have it like that, but you shouldn't hold that against me," I said, thinking I was wasting my time.

"Ok, I'm sorry if this is all coming across the wrong way. Just do me the pleasure of coming over for a study date," he said, getting on one knee.

"Get up boy!" I said, blushing. "I will see you tomorrow, but I reserve the right to treat to dinner if the food isn't good."

3 | Elephant in the Room

Have you ever had a day that was an endless string of surprises? My "study date" with Marc was just that kind of day. It started with an unexpected text message from my brother, Maurice, telling me he wanted to stop and see me on his return trip home. His group performed at a lounge in North Carolina, and he would pass me on the way back to D.C. I did not mind seeing him, it was the other baggage that came along with him. He was one of a three-member boy group, which started when they were in college. They all had an epiphany at the same time that they were going to drop out of school and pursue their careers full-time. This epiphany just so conveniently happened when Maurice got his first payment from my father's estate.

They had a manager named Jesse who gave me the creeps. He was in his 40s, good-looking, married, father of three children, owned a barber shop, and supposedly managed other R&B groups. Nevertheless, there was something about him that didn't quite sit well with me. Maurice and his guy friends were no doubt all Fruit Loops, and Jesse was their manager. What heterosexual man would want to babysit three young gay guys? They all called him Dad, which angered me hearing my brother call another dude Dad. Maurice told me that Jesse gave him the support both financially and otherwise that he needed. He said Jesse believed in him so, to him, he was his father. That bovine scat probably made my father turn upside down in his grave.

"Fatima, open the door. I have to pee," Maurice exclaimed like he was dying.

When I opened the door, my high-yellow, frailly thin brother stood with his eyebrows perfectly arched, his cheekbones chiseled like a painting, his hair flawless, and his expensive clothes.

"You know there are things called restrooms located in gas stations and fast food restaurants that travelers can use while on the road," I said, letting him in.

"Yuck, I would never," he said, walking back to my bathroom like a damn Diva. Then there was a playful knock on my door.

"Hi, Fatima," Jesse said, undressing me with his eyes.

"Hi, Jesse," I replied not knowing whether to shut the door in his face or barf.

"Where is the nearest mall? I told the boys I would attempt to do some shopping while you and Mo bonded," he said like he was taking his children out while letting me have a play date with one of them.

"Up the street, a couple of miles on your right," I replied, closing the door in his face.

"OMG," Maurice said as he picked up a bottle of Remy I had left over from my party.

"What do you know about that?" I asked, becoming increasingly curious.

"That's my shit," he said, trying to sound hard.

"Well, it was left over from my party, and I don't like it. Someone bought it for me," I said, noticing that my brother was more fragile than he was the last time I saw him during Christmas.

"Why are you losing weight?" I asked, hoping he wasn't out there having unprotected sex.

"It's so stressful. When we're not in the studio, we're on the road. Our show last night was the shit! It was insane; bitches were throwing their panties at us," he said with a half-smile.

"Are you ok, Maurice?" I asked, looking past the fake smile.

"Well, I was wondering if I could hold ten stacks for a couple of months? I promise I will pay you back when I get my next check," he said, trying to hug me.

"What do you need $10,000 for?" I asked, pushing his arms off me.

"We're making a music video, and we were short on money, so I told the guys that I would help out," he said.

"What about Jesse? He is your manager. He is supposed to take care of these matters for you all," I furthered in my interrogation.

"Dad already does a lot for the guys and me," he said before I cut him off.

"Stop calling that weirdo Dad! You had a father, and he is dead. Jesse is not your fucking father," I vented.

"Fuck our father! He wasn't a father to me! He didn't do shit with me or for me. All he cared about was his fucking career, image, and hoes!"

"Well, then stop receiving his money!" I replied because I couldn't refute what he had stated.

"His money? That is the least he could do!" he said with tears in his eyes.

"I don't have $10,000 to give you," I said, changing the subject.

"Ok, are you kidding me? That's five pairs of shoes for you. I said a loan, but whatever," he said as he began texting Jesse to pick him up.

"So, I guess that was it! You just came to hit me up for money?" I asked, becoming angry and feeling used once again.

"What else is there Fatima? You are so much like him. You don't support me! You only care about yourself!"

"Wow, I am like Dad? Well, maybe I am! Yes, I take pride in making my own money! I don't go around bumming money off people. I don't go masquerading like I am something that I am not!" I said, releasing my anger.

"Who is masquerading?" he began.

"You are Maurice! You come in here wearing Gucci this and Tom-you-can't-a-Ford but asking me for $10,000. You look like you weigh a hundred pounds and smell like you bathed in weed and alcohol last night. You talk about bitches throwing their panties at you when it is evident that you only like boxers!" I said it and regretted it all at the same time.

He looked shocked as if I let the cat out the bag and put his hands over his face.

"You're gay Maurice! It's about time someone addressed the elephant in the room. And you have a substance abuse problem," I said just getting it all out.

I felt like I was wrong in saying it because I was angered by him comparing me to our father. I wanted to hurt him, but when I saw him crying a part of me began to hurt. Regardless of his choices, he was my brother. I went over to him to give him comfort, but he rejected me.

"Don't touch me! You are a fucking hypocrite! You want to keep it real, then let's go there. Like I said, you are your father's daughter. He was a hoe, and so are you! I'm the one who was left at home with Mama while you two freaks were out fucking half of DC. I'm surprised you two didn't fuck each other," he said, grabbing my hand as I went to slap him.

"Whatever I am is none of your business, but do know this bitch, I am a virgin! I know that word sounds like Chinese to your ass. You fuck for Red Bottoms like a dog does tricks for bones. It doesn't matter how red the bottom of your shoes is when your soul is black. Next time you want to take someone to the dumpster, make sure you dump your trash first, Becky-with-the-permed-hair," Maurice said, trying to leave my apartment, but I grabbed him by his shoulder.

"Well, your father loved this permed-hair whore more than his frail faggot son. Did it ever dawn on you that maybe the reason he stayed gone was you? That he couldn't stomach having a gay son. I'd rather give $5 blow jobs and eat at soup kitchens than be you. I may have trash in my dumpster, but you are the dumpster. I wish Mom would have miscarried you! Now, get the fuck out of my home!" I yelled with tears streaming down my face.

"I wish she would have too, and then I wouldn't have you as a sister. I hope the next time I see you is in a cemetery," he said, slamming the door so hard that it re-opened.

What could I say? He spoke the truth; I was my father's daughter. Hard words to hear but very true nevertheless; if promiscuity was a gene, then I guess I inherited it from my father. The major difference between him and me was I did not cheat. I can remember countless times throughout my life feeling the awkwardness between my parents especially when certain women were around.

I had my suspicions but never any concrete evidence until one night when we hosted a Christmas party at our home for my father's colleagues and friends. I was looking for a place to sneak off with Andrew, my father's business partner's son. We were just going to do our usual kissing, grinding, and oral sex. So, we went to my brother's room, only to find Andrew's mother bent over with my father screwing her from behind. I guess everyone's nut was messed up that night.

My father left home for a couple of months, I guess, as some pseudo punishment. With his partnership destroyed, he went into a private practice by himself. I never saw Andrew again which was probably for the best. I knew my mother would take my father back because she would not want the moniker of a single mother. My mother cared about status and image more than anything else in the world, probably even more than her children.

I had to do something to shake the tension of the argument off me, so I called Charles. Unfortunately, his phone picked up and I was privy to a conversation between him and a patient.

"I got back your paperwork, and everything looks good," he said when she cut him off.

"Yes, it does. It looks really good," she said, sounding like a white girl.

"Hold on, let me lock this," he said.

Then there was silence for a second until I heard him moaning. I heard some obscure sounds that ended when he came.

"Mmm...You taste so delicious Charles," she said, making me want to throw up.

She had given him head during her annual visit. My level of irritation went through the roof.

"Anything to make a good patient happy," he replied as if this was their norm.

"Go to the front, and Candra will set you up for your next appointment in six months," he said like business as usual.

"I wish I didn't have to wait so long but what can a girl do? Oh, how I envy your wife. She gets to feel it in her. Oh well, beggars can't be choosy, but if you ever need something different, just call me," she said.

My heart felt like it was shattered into a million pieces as I hung up. Should I expect a cheater to be faithful? I know I was a hypocrite, but I desperately wanted to believe his lie about me being the only one. I needed someone to love me. Before I could get lost in my thoughts, my phone rang. It was Charles. He asked if I called and I said yes and told him it went to voicemail. He tried to make small talk, but I shut it down when I told him I was on my way to a date. I wanted him to know I had other options too. No more playing Ms.-Nice-Side-Chick!

When I arrived at Marc's, I was slightly inebriated to numb some of the pain from the day's activities. I didn't know what I was walking into, but it couldn't be worse than what I had just experienced.

"What happened to you today or should I dare ask?" Marc inquired, hugging me cautiously.

It felt so good to feel arms around me that I squeezed him a little more than what I should have. Before I knew it, hot tears covered my face. I thought about my conversation with Maurice and how I was like my father. When I tried to detach from Marc, I began thinking about Charles. I was a fool to think that a liar could be true. The worst feeling was to think I was to blame for it all.

"Fatima, it is going to be alright. Whatever you are going through, in time it will get better. If it is another dude, we come a dime a dozen and can be replaced easily," he said, holding my chin with one hand and wiping my tears with his other hand.

"I'm sorry Marc," I said, breaking free and grabbing some tissues from my purse.

"Don't be. Everyone has a bad day. Everyone has a breaking point," he said, trying to comfort me.

"I'm not the emotional type though. I don't want you to get the wrong impression of me. I am not that whimpering chick; I can take a lot," I said, trying to reassure him I was not fragile as if I should've even cared what he thought.

"Sometimes it's great to break the monotony. Try something new. There is no special award given to those who are strong 24-7," he smiled, escorting me into his living room.

"Wow, she is pretty!" I said, looking at pictures of his daughter, Madison, throughout the place.

"Why thank you! I think she gets some of it from me," he smiled with great pride.

"She's your clone, but prettier," I laughed for the first time.

"I like your smile," he said with a boyish grin.

"Better than me putting makeup and snot all over your shirt," I said, looking at my foundation and eyeliner all over his white shirt, hoping he wasn't repulsed.

"I kinda like it. It adds personality to this plain old white shirt. But I like your tears too," he said with a more serious tone.

"You like seeing people in pain?" I asked a bit askance.

"I like seeing the real person. I appreciate smiles but also appreciate tears. I love a beautifully made face, but I love waking to a bare one. I love when everything is nice and neat, and I love when there are a couple of things out of place," he said, staring at me intensely.

"Whoa, that is deep. I have never heard anyone say that before. That's very conscious coming from a guy," I said still in awe.

"I am not like any guy you have ever met before," he said, sounding like a broken record.

"My experiences show me that every guy who has uttered that self-righteous claim is often accurate. They are not like any guy I have met before because they have another degree or hue of bullshit I have never been exposed to previously," I said, wondering why I came to his place.

"Ok, you will see. I'll tell you this, I'm better than Jasper!" he boasted.

"That's not saying much; Jasper is a whore! There are stray dogs walking around alleys in heat that are better than Jasper," I laughed.

"Wow! You hit hard! So why were you with him?" he asked.

"Because I knew exactly what I was getting. I wasn't looking for a relationship," I smirked.

"Well, you will see I am true blue" he reaffirmed.

"What makes you so sure of yourself? You act like this is on your resume," I said, becoming intrigued.

"I have a daughter, mother, sisters, aunts, exes, and female friends. I am a woman expert. Most of the time, they seek me out for advice. Sometimes, it's better to get advice about men from a man," he said as if he was schooling me.

"Okay, duly noted. So, are you dating anyone right now?" I asked, cutting to the chase.

"Nothing serious. I am still ebbing and flowing through baby-mama-drama. I don't want anyone to have to deal with that until I can fully deal with it. What about you?"

"The same, nothing serious. So, you have a lot of female friends?" I asked.

He grabbed his cell and opened his Facebook account.

"Here are some of my homegirls. This is Rachel; she is like a kid sister to me," he said, pointing to a cute Hispanic looking girl.

"What is she, Hispanic? Are you sure you don't have any incestuous feelings for Rachel or any buried feelings for your homegirls?" I asked jokingly but quite suspicious.

"No, she's Aruban. And boy, you must have been dicked over by someone or someones. No, a friend is a friend. I don't have feelings for my friends, plus most of them are not even my type."

"Oh, what is your type? Please do tell," I became increasingly alert.

"I have had a preference for exotic girls, like Hispanic, Asian, or a mixture," he added as if he was talking about a food menu.

"Well, I don't fit that description, but your daughter's mom and even your kid sister, Rachel, do," I added, turning on the flame. I didn't know how to feel about his statement. Was he trying something new? Was he settling with me because who he wanted didn't want him?

"Just a preference, but nothing serious. Beautiful has no box, and you are beautiful. What is your preference?" he asked, almost making me want to lie, but I told him the truth.

"You. Tall, dark, and handsome. However, I have never met a dark-skinned man who knows the meaning of fidelity," I answered, throwing shade at him for his exotic preference.

"I could take that the wrong way, but I won't bother. Consider yourself lucky. Today is the day you have met a faithful dark-skinned man. I am the type of guy every girl wants to take home to meet their parents," he said before we sat down to eat dinner.

He was far from a chef, but I loved the fact that he tried. I guess women parallel men in some ways. Men are enamored with the chase more so than the catch. Women are more enamored with the effort rather than the result. Men get high on performing, and we get high on seeing them perform.

Although I had certain red flags about Marc, I thought what could I lose by trying something new? He seemed like a nice guy, nothing too extra yet not too plain. I felt so at ease with him that I allowed him to seduce me that night. He wasn't the best, but he wasn't the worse. When it was over, I was ready to go home. He did not stop me but did mention that our next date would be a movie I wanted to see.

4 | The Newness

From that night, things progressed between Marc and I in turtle steps. At times, I didn't know what to think. Some days there were endless streams of texts from him, and other days, I wouldn't hear from him. Sometimes, he would have short, keeping-in-touch conversations when he was with female friends, and other times late at night, he would call me and talk for hours. I was beginning to see a pattern of inconsistency. I finally voiced it when he invited me back over for a booty call under the disguise of "just chilling." When we finished, and I turned to get my earrings off his nightstand, I saw two stubs of a movie we were supposed to see together. I was going to remain silent, but I couldn't.

"So, you finally made it to the movie," I said, lifting up the stubs.

"Oh yeah," he replied.

"Who did you see it with?" I inquired when I realized he went the day after my first visit to his place.

"I don't remember," he replied.

"You can't remember who you went to the movies with two weeks ago? The night after you screwed me," I said, becoming annoyed.

We weren't in a relationship, but I didn't feel like dealing with another liar. I just wanted to deal with a man who would own his truth, whatever that was.

"I think Rachel. Yeah, I paid, and she used her student ID," he said suddenly being cured of amnesia.

"Did you realize that it was the movie you said you would take me to? Or was that just to be nice since you screwed me," I asked, trying to push his buttons.

"Are we in a relationship? Did I miss the memo? Why so many questions and speculation?" he asked like a quintessential asshole.

"You know what, you are so right. We are nothing. I just inquired since you said you were different. But, now that I know you are just like any other dude, then it makes it easier," I said, grabbing my purse to leave.

"Easier for what? You're not leaving, are you?" he said, coming in between me and the door.

"Easier for these words to come out of my mouth. Kiss the most exotic place on my yellow ass. Now, move out of my way!" I yelled.

"Are you freaking serious? Are you kidding me? Don't even go there! How am I supposed to take you seriously when you were sexing my friend who you admitted is a dog? Then, you say how you're such a tough chick and not weak to men. What are one night and some conversations with a guy like me? I am not even your regular type. I'm not an older, successful baller. Because I went to a damn movie with my friend who is like a sister to me, you are shitting on me?" he asked, moving out the way and opening the door.

"Jasper was nothing to me; he is your friend. That is your issue, not mine. You are a sneaky bastard that loves swiping your friend's leftovers," I vented.

"So, you are his leftovers? Thanks for telling me. You wanted to be with him and were using me as a second. You were probably taking notes while we were having sex," he said, sounding pathetic.

"Is that why your dick couldn't stay hard," I said, slamming the door. I didn't want his neighbors to know all my business.

"I told you, it takes a couple of times for me because I am not like other guys. I don't usually have sex with women with whom I don't have an emotional connection. I'm sorry I let you down," he said, looking wounded.

"I don't care. It didn't mean anything anyway," I said finally calming down.

"To who? It meant something to me. I can't stop thinking about you. I try not calling you because I don't want to be another dude who is sweating you. I think about you all the time even when I try not to. When I talk to Jasper, it is awkward because I want to say something, but then I don't want to overstep my boundaries with you. I just feel confused, and I am sorry if that is coming across as if I don't care because that is the last thing I want you to believe. I care a lot," he said, kissing my forehead.

I was in complete shock. Was he gaming me? He looked and sounded so sincere.

"Let's start over! I am not the best at showing how I feel so give me another chance," he smiled.

"I guess," I said, trying to end the conversation.

"You were trying to break up with me before you met my folks and my daughter," he said, grabbing my hand and pulling me close to him.

"What are you talking about?" I inquired.

"I want you to meet them at graduation. Is that cool with you?" he asked.

"I guess so," I answered, feeling awkward because we weren't in a committed relationship.

"How do you feel about marrying someone who has children?" he asked, throwing me completely through a loop.

"I have dated someone who has children," I answered.

"I said marrying not dating?" he clarified.

"I guess it depends on the person and our situation," I answered, hoping he would change the conversation.

"Do you consider children as baggage?" he insisted.

"No, but I consider their mothers baggage. I don't know if I can stomach baby-mama-drama. I will cuss a bitch out," I said with no hesitation.

"Do you want to have children?" he asked.

"Absolutely!" I replied.

"Wow, you said that with great certainty," he said, looking at me in awe.

"Why? I don't seem like the maternal type?" I asked.

"Your hips do!" he laughed. "Not really. You seem like the independent woman who doesn't want marriage or children."

"Well, you don't seem like the marrying type either. However, I didn't say anything about marriage; I said I wanted children."

"Children, but no marriage. Why not marriage?" he asked.

"Let's say I have trust issues. I don't want to get a divorce," I answered, thinking about my parents.

"Your parents didn't divorce, so why do you think you would?" he probed deeper.

"But they should have. Why stay married and pretend? I don't want to pretend. With children, you don't have to pretend to love them. They are your flesh and blood. You can't divorce them," I said, giving him more transparency than I had intended.

"Apples and oranges comparison. Children don't come into the world loving you rather needing you. Your children can't love you, well at least not how a real man can," he said, staring deeply into my eyes.

"Well, children can't hurt you as a man can. Anyway, I don't know if I have met a real man," I said, returning his stares.

"How about your first love, Andrew?" he asked, lessening the tension between us.

"That was puppy love, and I have my parents to thank for that heartbreak," I said, reliving a dark moment from my past.

"So, you did love him?" he asked.

"I guess. He was my first, and he made me feel like I mattered. But, then my Dad messed that up and then," I said, stopping myself.

"Then what?' he asked.

"No, I'm good," I said, trying to end the conversation.

"How can I get to know you better when you won't let me in," he insisted.

"You are in. Didn't we just have sex?" I rebutted.

"I want in your heart," he said, catching me off guard.

"You shouldn't go places that you don't know how to do the upkeep or repair," I said, hoping he would halt.

"I may not be a doctor, but I can treat your heart better," he said, grabbing my hand. "Let me in. Let me love you."

"Love? What do you know about love?" I said as tears began to fill my eyes.

"I am a father and having my daughter taught me how to love selflessly," he said, rubbing my cheek.

"About a month after my father was caught cheating, I told my mother my period didn't come. She sent me to my father's office. He had me pee in a cup. About twenty minutes later, he had me put on a gown and took me into another room. He put a mask on my face. I woke up about what seemed minutes later, and one of his nurses gave me a pad. I thought, wow, my dad made me have my period. It wasn't until a month later I overheard him and my mother arguing that I found out he performed a D&C at the request of my mother so she wouldn't be embarrassed about having a pregnant teenage daughter."

"I'm sorry Fatima. I didn't know," he said, reaching to hug me.

"It's all good. Maybe it was for the best. Andrew's parents and mine never spoke again, and his parents eventually divorced," I said, remembering those turbulent times.

"The next time I was pregnant was by my boyfriend in college. We didn't know I was pregnant because I still had my cycle. I was pledging when I miscarried, so they performed an emergency D&C on me.

Probably was for the best because shortly after, I found out he was screwing some white girl," I said, once again reliving my painful past.

"Wow, you mentioned you had some abortions, but I didn't know these painful stories. I am so sorry. Lynelle and I had an abortion also, but she refused to have one with Madison, and I am glad we didn't," he smiled.

"I believe I could be a good single parent," I said, imagining just raising my children by myself.

"No such luck if we got pregnant," he said, throwing me off guard.

"If we got pregnant we wouldn't keep it," I said before I even had time to think. "But, hopefully, we won't have to worry about that."

"No, we would get married," he said, shocking me.

"Marriage? Are you serious? I can't see that," I said, being as honest as I could. "You're a nice guy but…"

"I'm a nice guy but what? I'm not rich. I don't look like a model. I don't come from the who's who," he ranted.

"We just met, and we barely know each other. Please stop bringing up that other bullshit. I hate that," I said, once again turned off by his insecurities.

"Well, give us a chance, Fatima," Marc said, pulling me toward him.

I felt awkward yet flattered at the same time. Was he serious? He was hard to read, but deep inside I needed a reprieve from my life as is. I needed to build a better landscape than what I presently had. Giving Marc a chance was a gamble but what did I have to lose?

I deserved to experience someone new. I hoped he was this different species of man he proclaimed to be. He placed my hand on his chest.

"Do you feel my heartbeat?" he asked.

I could, and it was beating strongly.

"Let me love you," he said, putting his tongue carefully into my mouth.

He grabbed my breast and slowly took off my bra. He sucked and slightly grazed his teeth around my hard nipples. He held both of my hands as he slowly kissed my stomach down to my inner thigh. He teased around my vagina but would not touch it. Then he picked me up and carried me to his room.

I began to undress, but he stopped me.

"Don't, I want to undress you. Lay down," he said, as he undressed in front of me.

He slowly rubbed himself and looked at me. I became more excited with expectation. He then took off my thong.

"Now, play with it. Let me see how you make her happy," he said, sitting on his knees still rubbing himself.

I began masturbating before him, and then he took the tip and began to slide it up and down my slit. I really wanted him to just put all of it in me in one big motion, but he teased me. Then he turned me on my stomach and put a wet finger in my butt, but I jumped. He took the hint that that area was forbidden, so he thrust into me while he played with me. He kissed my neck and ears while he penetrated and fondled me. When we came, he uttered the words, "I love you."

5 | Troubled Waters

The newness of anything somehow has a way of taking people on momentary sabbaticals from the real world. Life felt good. I landed a dynamic summer internship in DC, Marc and I became an item, and my best friend, Giselle, was in love.

"He is almost unbelievable! He is a gentleman; he hasn't pressured me for sex or even brought up the topic. He makes the sweetest little gestures to let me know he is thinking about me," she beamed with joy.

"I am not surprised. John seems like a true-blue; the kind you take home to your mother," I said, being reminded of Marc's statement about himself.

"Graduation is in two days, and I get to meet his parents. I am so nervous! You are meeting Marc's parents, right?" she asked while grabbing her cell phone.

"Yes. I will meet them and his daughter," I said, wondering what was in store for me.

"Aww, it's John. He texted me that he is taking me to dinner tomorrow night to meet his parents and sister," she said, jumping up and down.

To think, she was deeply enamored with a guy she had never had sex with and is now meeting his family. Her glow was undeniable, and I believed she deserved it; she was a *good girl*, the type that deserved good shit to happen to them. I, on the other hand, knew Marc about the same time Giselle knew John and we were sexing every moment that we could. We hadn't been on an official date. I guess there was no need to wine and dine me given that he already got the prize.

"So, what are you going to wear to dinner tomorrow night to meet the Andersons?" I asked, trying to share her excitement while still second-guessing my relationship.

"I don't know, but something conservative. I don't want to show too much," Giselle said, going through her closet.

"You will look great in anything Giselle. Look, I have a question for you. Does John have close female friends?" I asked, thinking about all of Marc's *sister-friends*.

"No, not really. I asked about his friends, and he said Quincy and Donald, his best friend from high school and a couple of other dudes," she said as if she was trying to recount in her mind.

"Interesting! Do you know if he has an opinion about guys who have several female friends?" I asked, becoming a little annoyed with thoughts of some of Marc's clandestine behavior.

"Well, he said not too many guys want to be friends with females. They are usually put in the friend or brother category by women who don't want to sex them. What's up?" she inquired.

"Marc has a lot of "friends" that are like his little sisters. However, I get the feeling that they are only *sisters* because they put him in that category, to John's point. There is one, in particular, this Hispanic chick that I heard was a hoe. One day, while I was visiting, she came to see him with some spandex pants on with a camel toe and a sports bra. She said she was visiting her friend that lives in his complex. She and Marc supposedly have been friends forever," I said, still remembering details of that day.

"You don't trust him. Do you think they have had more?" she asked.

"I don't mean to rain on your parade," I said, offering to end the conversation.

"No, it's good to talk to someone to get another perspective," she said, sitting next to me.

"When she left, he went outside after her and spoke for about ten minutes. That pissed me off as I thought why the hell they couldn't talk in front of me. While he was gone, he received a call from one of his guy friends. When I scrolled his call log, I saw phone calls between Rachel and him, sometimes even right after or before he called me. It even appeared that sometimes he ended our conversations or wouldn't answer mine to talk to her," I said, becoming vulnerable.

Was I an idiot for trying to believe in Marc?

"Well, did you ask him about it?" she asked already knowing the answer.

"Is my name Fatima Antoinette Crosby? Then he got defensive and flipped the script. He made an issue of me violating his privacy, then saying how I don't trust him, and finally how he can't seem to keep me happy," I said, reliving it all again.

"Well, is it all true?" she asked.

"Yes, there is something about him. Although he seems like a regular old nice guy, he is secretive, and his behavior is inconsistent. When our argument got heated, I said Rachel was dressed like a hoe like she was on the prowl seeing what or who she could get. He seemed wounded and said she and I have similar tastes in clothing. We fought, and I left. That is why I am not so excited about meeting his people. I haven't spoken to him for a week. For all I know, he's been fucking someone else," I said, finally getting it off my chest.

"A relationship without trust is no relationship at all. If you have a gut feeling, go with it. It is your intuition, and it won't steer you wrong for the most part," Giselle said, hugging me.

Sometimes you just need to hear someone confirm that which you already know to be true. Half of me wanted to believe Marc, and the other half of me wanted to jump ship as soon as possible. I was already too familiar with disappointment and heartbreak. In my new relationship with Marc, I shared about Charles to build trust. I did not make it a habit of disclosing my love life to guys I was dating, but since I wanted transparency from him, I decided to put my foot first. The most I received from him was his admitting he had a temper and sometimes broke things. I asked if he was faithful to Madison's mother, and he said he was not the cheater. I did not know if that meant not a cheater now, then, or in general. Nonetheless, he shared that she cheated on him, which of course raised my eyebrow. Most women don't cheat, and I wondered what he did to warrant that. It must have been bad. Most men cheat just to get ass; most women cheat to get affection and attention that they are not getting from their men.

Every so often when we got into arguments, he would bring Charles up and in return, I would throw in his baby's mama. I knew there was no way I could have a future with this boy; he was so far from being the kind of man I wanted to marry, which was closer to Charles, who I abruptly deleted out of my life. He called, texted, emailed, and Facebooked me for months, but I did not respond. Nonetheless, he wasn't a doctor because of his good looks. The eve of Marc's graduation, I got a surprise visitor.

"Are you serious?" I asked, opening my bedroom door. Amanda let him in not knowing our history.

"Hi, Fatima," he said, looking through my soul.

"Fatima, I'm gone. I'll be back Sunday night," Amanda said, leaving.

This was one of the rare times I wished she stayed.

"Why are you here?" I asked, still in complete shock about him being in Charlottesville in my apartment.

"I somehow lost my heart, and my GPS told me it was here," he said, still staring at me with a grave look.

"You didn't have to come down here to find your heart. Just unzip your pants! You have the biggest heart I know, and you don't mind sharing it with everyone!" I said, coming out of my room.

"What are you talking about? I have not had sex with anyone else other than you, not even my wife. Fatima, I love you," he said, trying to reach for me.

"Maybe, I am every bit of my age and was naïve enough to think a cheater could be faithful, but I know the truth now. I'm done, Charles. Don't you have a patient waiting to suck your dick," I said, going for the jugular?

He stared at me dumbfounded.

"What, cat got your damn tongue?" I asked.

"There's nothing I can say, but I am so sorry," he said, putting his head down.

"Yes, you are! Very sorry! There are tons of women waiting for you in DC to receive your benevolence. Let's not keep them waiting," I said, walking to the door.

"Wait, baby. I love you and only you. Here," he said, handing me a large manila envelope.

"What is this?" I said, grabbing it from his hands. It was separation papers that dated back to February, a month after my birthday.

"I have moved out and only see the children on the weekends," he said, torturing my heart and mind with the question if he did this for me.

"Well, I wish you well! I am in a committed relationship," I said, trying to end this surprise visit.

"Ha! Are you kidding me?" He vented.

"No, I'm serious! What, you think nobody wants me?" I asked.

"I don't want any nigga putting his hands on you unless it's to operate. Even then, they have to get my damn permission!" he yelled.

"And why?" I asked

"Because, this right here belongs to me," he said, walking up to me and grabbing my vagina.

"Get your damn hands off of me you whore!" I yelled, slapping his hand away. "Get out of my apartment!"

"I love you, Fatima! What about that don't you understand? And the thought of some random nigga fucking my pussy makes me want to kill someone," he said, slapping his hand on my table.

"Oh, so all I am is some pussy! It's ok for you to screw half of DC, but let me have not a hook-up but a real relationship, and now you have all this emotion. You are a hypocrite!" I said, walking toward the door again.

"Baby," he said in a calmer voice, reaching out to me. "You can't love him, and even if you think you do, he is probably not on the level of what you need," he said as if he were the Fatima expert.

"Oh, that's right, and you would know exactly what I need. A broken heart, broken promises, and whorish asshole who fucks half of DC under the auspices of being an OB-GYN," I said, spewing venom and hoping to wound him so that this episode could be over.

"Say what you want. You have a right. Yes, I have gotten my dick sucked by a couple of women, patients, and non-patients. But, I did not put my dick in them. It may be all the same to you, but at the time, it wasn't for me. What I want is to end this madness. I want my heart and my mind to be one. I need and want you, Fatima," he said, walking near me. His words, which at one time would have healed me, were masticating my very soul.

"What I need is for you to go," I said, opening the door, only to find Marc. Damn! Damn! Damn!

Our faces changed in a flash. My face morphed from anger to shock. Marc's face changed from sullen to anger. Charles face turned from pain to joy. He had everything to gain in this situation. Marc and I hadn't spoken since our argument that stemmed from Rachel. We both were stubborn, which was probably our biggest challenge. Now to add wood to the fire, here we stood in my apartment with the man I told him I had been madly in love with, who embodied the characteristics of everything Marc wasn't.

"Come in. Charles was just leaving," I said, motioning for Charles to exit.

"Hello brother, my name is Dr. Charles Chappelle," he said, extending his hand and delaying his stay.

Marc said nothing but walked right by him and sat on my couch. He stared at me with piercing eyes like a volcano about to erupt.

"I want you to think about what I said. The offer still stands, and it should be the only one worth considering," Charles said, leaving. I couldn't slam the door fast enough. I knew that last statement was going to give me hell to pay for with Marc.

"What the fuck!" Marc yelled, slamming a glass of water on my coffee table onto the wall. I would have been appalled and frightened, but I had witnessed his temper tantrums previously.

"Look, don't come in my place breaking shit! You can leave, just like he did. I haven't heard from you in over a week…"

"So, you start screwing that motherfucker again? I don't believe this," he said, pacing back and forth.

"What I don't believe is that you even believe that. If I was, why would I tell Charles to leave and you to stay? This is what I am talking about! You act like a damn child instead of…"

"Instead of a smug OB-GYN! I saw how that asshole looked at me like I wasn't shit. Then his last words about you not really having any other options. I should have punched him in his face," he said, punching a hole in my wall.

"What? Marc, get out of here now! I have to pay for that," I screamed in shock.

"That's all you care about! My fucking heart is bleeding, and you care about a damn wall. I will pay for it," he said with hot tears streaming down his face. He threw a wad of hundred-dollar bills on my table.

"That's all I have right now. If you need more, let me know," he said, sitting on the floor with his head in between his knees.

I was so angry. I didn't know whether to comfort him or throw him out. What had I gotten myself into? I went from a man with no dick control to a boy with no self-control. Yes, Marc was different like he claimed to be, but in a negative way. He was a different species of the same genus, LOSERS. What was it like to be with a *nice guy*? Did they exist? It seemed like they were only meant for girls like Giselle. Nice girls meet nice guys, which meant I was shit.

"I'll get that," Marc said as he grabbed the glass I was picking up.

"I don't like to lose control like that, but," he began to say, but I cut him off.

"Have you ever put your hands on a woman?" I asked, sure of the answer.

"No, never!" he said, and I knew he had to be lying.

"Well, let's be clear. If you ever put your hands on me, I am pressing charges. No ifs, ands, or buts about it," I said, looking directly into his eyes.

"You seem like the type," he replied, as he cleaned the mess he made.

I wanted to probe into what his statement meant, but I left well enough alone. He was what he was. I did not see a future with him, and there was no need going places with him mentally or emotionally that would avail nothing.

"I did not have sex with Charles. He did a surprise visit, just like you," I said, explaining as if I owed him an excuse.

"Then you come over here unannounced after almost two weeks of silence and a few texts talking about how you miss me."

"Excuse me; I didn't know I had to ask for permission to come to my girl's crib. It won't happen again," he said, sounding like a child, which repulsed me.

"You haven't been acting like I'm your girl. What have you been doing?"

"Trying to get my head together and getting ready for graduation. My people are in town. That is why I stopped by to ask if you wanted to come with us to dinner," he said barely looking at me.

"I would have but under different circumstances. I will meet them tomorrow after graduation, right?" I asked politely declining his offer.

"Sure," he said as he kissed my forehead and left.

A million thoughts flooded my mind all at once. There was something different about Marc, and I couldn't put my hands on it. I was confused whether Charles' trip to see me was a ploy or sincerity. My mother wanted me to come up the weekend of her birthday, which meant seeing Maurice, who I hadn't seen or spoken to since our fight. Then, the cherry on top was meeting Marc's family tomorrow and pretending to be happy with him when that was the farthest thing from the truth.

During graduation, I sat with Giselle, who was gleaming with joy because her man was valedictorian of the graduating class. He also was president of the class, so he gave one speech for both honors. She told me that they became committed the night before while I had drama with Charles and Marc. That's how life is; while someone is crying, someone else is smiling. I was happy for her and I hoped their relationship would last.

When everything was over, I said goodbye to Giselle and made my way to Marc and his family. When I walked up to them, Rachel was hugging him.

"Everyone this is Rachel," he said, shocking me.

If they were such great friends, and she was like his sister for so long, why did she not know his family?

"Hi, Rachel. Where is your girlfriend, Fatima?" his mother smiled briefly at Rachel and then directly back to Marc.

"Hi everyone," I said with the biggest smile I could muster.

"Come here, honey. You must be Fatima" his mother said, extending her arms to me. I hugged her and his father.

"We finally get to meet you. Your pictures do you no justice. You are very pretty, and I love your outfit. She is a keeper," she winked at Marc. For a fleeting moment, I thought, *but is your son?*

"And this must be Madison. Hi, my name is Fatima," I said, bending down to greet Marc's daughter.

"You are pretty. You're daddy's girlfriend?" she blushed.

"Yeah, something like that," I smiled.

"Hi, Fatima," Rachel said, giving me a tight hug. You would have thought we were besties.

"You look wonderful, girl," she said, but I couldn't think of a compliment to give back. Instead of looking like a hoe, now she was looking like a nun, homely.

"I have to go, but it was nice meeting all of you," Rachel said, giving Marc another hug.

Marc's family paid for a pavilion where we had a catered barbeque. I liked that they were good old down-to-earth people, not the least bit pretentious. Now and then, he would check on me to see if I was alright and kiss me on my forehead. As the day progressed and I enjoyed his family, especially his mother, I slowly released the anger I had toward him.

"Fatima, I have heard great things about you. You seem to come from a good family and have some great goals. Just the type of young lady Marc needs to keep him on track," his father said.

"He's done a pretty good job, look at today," I said, stating the obvious.

"This wasn't a choice. His father and I got tired of bailing him out both literally and figuratively," she smiled, assuming I knew what she was talking about.

"This is the best thing he has done in a long time besides Madison," his father looked away as if he was recounting the past.

"Yes, but at the time you didn't feel that way," his mother added.

"Well, what parent is proud of their children having children without being married and not financially capable of taking care of them? Both bring too much, as your generation says, *baby mama drama*", his father said, looking at me.

"You don't have any children, right?" his mother inquired.

"No, ma'am. Got too much to do career-wise," I replied, thinking about the information Marc's parents was disclosing.

"Great! Stay focused. I would feel the same if I were in your shoes," his mother continued in her thoughts.

"I just don't know why these kids don't use birth control," his father added, shaking his head.

"Fatima, do you have any siblings?" his mother asked, jumping subjects again.

"Yes, one brother," I said, thinking of Maurice.

"Your mother and father had the perfect combination, a boy and a girl. What does your brother do?" she asked.

"He's a singer," I responded, hoping she would change the conversation again.

"Does he have children?" she continued.

"No ma'am, neither one of us," I replied, feeling that this was the beginning of my interrogation about my family.

"What do your parents do, if you don't mind me asking?" she continued, surprising me because I thought Marc had already told them about my family.

"My father was a doctor, but he is deceased, and my mother was a doctor, but retired early," I answered still hoping to end this conversation.

"I am so sorry. I think Marc mentioned something about that. Our condolences," she said as if my loss was recent.

"It's been two years. Although it seems like yesterday, we are learning to live with it every day. So, how did you two meet?" I asked finally turning the conversation.

"We grew up together. She was my first girlfriend. We have been together since we were ten years old," his father said, surprising me.

"Wow, that is amazing!"

"Yes, we celebrate our 45th wedding anniversary next month. I am sure Marc told you about it," his mother replied.

"Oh yes," I lied, feeling that Marc had no plans of inviting me.

"What are you all talking about?" Marc asked as he finally came to check on me.

"You, of course," his mother rolled her eyes.

"Well, I hope not too much," he responded, looking at her intensely.

"Never too much," I smiled as I looked away.

"So, you are bringing Fatima to our vow renewal?" his father prodded.

"Yeah, about that, I guess you know that," he began but I cut him off.

"I would be delighted to, but I don't know my work schedule yet. I will be commuting to Atlanta this summer for my internship," I said, looking at his parents. Marc was such an asshole that I dared not look at him.

"We hope you can make it. Marc, we love Fatima. She is a keeper," his mother put her arm around me while looking at him.

But, did I want to be kept? The more I discovered about Marc, the more apprehensive I became about our relationship. Sometimes, I felt like we connected, and other times I felt like he was a complete stranger.

Imagine having a baby with someone who only showed you shades of who he is. I couldn't imagine it. From his graduation day forward, he played the role of the doting boyfriend. However, something in me was not at ease. I thought perhaps it was my hormones because I missed my cycle. Although I often skipped periods, this time it felt different, so I tested. I was pregnant. I felt like someone poured boiling hot water over me. Condoms and birth control were equally garbage!

"It won't be that bad. I mean, we didn't want it to be this way, but we can make the best out of it. I love you and want to marry you," Marc said, shocking me.

"Do you even know what you are saying right now?" I asked. I wasn't sure I wanted to marry him, and I definitely did not want to be connected to him because of a child.

"You are the best thing that has happened to me in a long time. I know I may have a messed-up way of showing it, but I do love you," he said, trying to convince me.

"Do you care what I want?" I asked, feeling a rip tide of emotion. "You just graduated, and I have one more year left of school. On top of that, I am about to start my summer internship in DC. You live in Maryland and…"

"And I don't want you to worry about all of that. Let's take it one step at a time. I love you, and I am going to do what I have to make this as painless as possible for you. Trust me, Fatima."

Being a single mother or married mother, abort or not to abort, were the thoughts flooding my mind. Did it make a difference? I didn't care what others thought. For me, there was only one person's opinion I cared about, and that was my mother's mom. Mama was my heart and probably the only person I loved without exception. I loved my father, but I hated his behavior. I loved my mother, but I hated her passivity. I loved my brother, but I hated his mediocrity. But Mama, I loved her with no *buts* only *because*. I loved her because she spoke the truth. I loved her because I could talk to her about anything. I loved her because she didn't judge me, and even when she disagreed with my decisions, she loved me. I loved her because she was strong and courageous. She kicked cancer's ass when it attacked her body. Although I didn't consider myself a spiritual person, I knew where I could find God in the Earth.

6 | Tipping Point

Once I finished the semester, Mama came to visit my mother, and despite nausea from morning sickness, I drove to Maryland. The trip from DC to PG County, which usually took little time, lasted forever because of how I was feeling. I was looking forward to seeing her, but not my mother and my brother. My mother was superficial, and my brother was too, in addition to being a liar and free-loader who just so happened to be gay. This was the first time we saw each other since our argument. Neither one of us reached out to the other.

When I arrived at my mother's secluded golf community, the gate was up, which was great, so I didn't have to announce my arrival. I parked behind my grandmother's fiery red Corvette Stingray. She was a classy, sporty woman who spent her 72nd birthday in Dubai for two weeks with her boyfriend. Mr. Jack was retired and widowed just like her and her first serious relationship since my grandfather died ten years prior. After the death of my grandfather, whose family was from Washington DC, Mama moved back to her birthplace, Houston, Texas. She met Mr. Jack at a church convention. When I asked her why was she willing to date Mr.

Jack she replied, "he has the three C's: Christ, character, and common sense."

Sometimes, it was hard to believe that Mama and my mother were related. Mama was a woman of substance and loved God, but my mother was pretentious and only went to church for status. I daresay my mother knew nothing about the Bible. However, my mother was probably more like my grandfather who was a part of the Black bourgeois of Washington, DC. Mama and he met in Atlanta, where he attended Morehouse, and she attended Spelman. Initially, she wouldn't allow him to take her out on a date for one year. He told me that is when he knew she was the one. He asked her to marry him on their second date. She accepted, but would not marry him until she graduated. Then, she moved to DC where she was a housewife and socialite while raising three daughters, of which my mother was the oldest. My aunts Celeste and Norma were more like my grandmother, spiritual and down to earth. Right before my grandparent's 40th wedding anniversary, my grandfather died, and five days later Aunt Norma, the youngest, died in a car accident. I was amazed by my grandmother's strength as she buried her husband and daughter.

As I entered the guest house, expecting to steal some moments with Mama without having to see Mother and Maurice, I caught her at the end of her phone conversation with Mr. Jack.

"You don't have to worry about that, Jack. Nothing would make me want to move back here," she said. "Well, guess who just blessed me with her presence? Fatima, Jack says hello."

"Hi, Mr. Jack," I mustered still feeling nauseous.

"She says hi, babe. I will call you later," she said. "Love you too!"

"Love?" I asked.

"L-O-V-E. Yes, ma'am," she replied, smiling.

I saw a sparkle in her eyes I had never seen.

"Mama, you seem like you are on cloud nine. How was your trip and are things getting serious with you and Mr. Jack?" I asked.

"The trip was full of interesting things to do and see. And to answer your second question, as serious as it needs to be for now," she said, blushing.

"Your nails look great!" I said, admiring her long nails with clear polish. Nothing fancy but it had been a couple of years since she wore clear polish because of the discoloration of her nails due to chemo.

"God is so good. He is a healer and a restorer," she replied, gleaming. "When your grandfather and Norma died, I didn't think things could get worse, but when I felt that lump, I saw darkness coming."

"You seemed so strong during the whole ordeal. Were you ever scared?" I asked, knowing that I would have been.

"Not really, if that was God's will for me to die from breast cancer, then so be it. However, I didn't believe that to be true. Greater is He that is on the inside of me than he that is in the world," she replied smiling. She repeated that saying throughout my life although I didn't know exactly what it meant.

"Then every day, I am reminded that I am a miracle when I see the scars where my breasts once were. I give God praise because His Son bore scars too!" she continued.

"Was it God or chemo that healed you, Mama?" I asked quite perplexed.

"Chemo is designed to kill. It kills cancer, and at the same time, it kills healthy cells too. However, baby, when the doctor says stage 4, that means it is finished. Death had metastasized throughout my body. You remember me weighing 80 pounds, right?" she asked still smiling.

"Yes, I was so scared of losing you," I said as tears filled my eyes.

"It was at my weakest that God was at His strongest and He showed out. Fatima, by faith we are healed. Jesus's blood trumped cancer's attack on my blood. Medical science is bewildered and utterly flabbergasted by my healing," she said, crying tears of joy.

"Wow, every time you speak about this I get chills. It's so surreal. But I was there and saw it with my own eyes. If that happened to me, well I guess I would just be dead," I said.

"Watch your words. Speak life, Fatima, never death," she said, rubbing my face.

"So, does Mr. Jack know about?" I hesitated.

"My breasts being removed and me opting not to replace them? Why, of course. You know your grandmother, I don't believe in keeping secrets. He has a right to know so he can choose whether that's something he can deal with or not," she said not blinking.

"What did he say?" I asked, hoping I wasn't overstepping my boundaries.

"He said he'd rather have the chest of a virtuous woman than the breasts of a whore," she laughed.

"Oh my God. Ok, Mr. Jack. It's like that!" I exclaimed, shocked by the answer.

"He doesn't mince his words, like me. I appreciate his candor," she replied.

"Do you ever feel like half a woman with no breasts?" I asked, knowing I would.

"I was a woman before I developed breasts. Wholeness has nothing to do with body parts rather mind and spirit. If your mind or spirit is cut or broken, then you may feel like a fractional person. If I allowed my mind to believe I am a fractional person because I don't have breasts, then that is what I would become. Jesus wants us to be W-H-O-L-L-Y as he is," she said, lifting her hands up.

"Well, I guess I better get my wholly self into the house and say hi to Mother," I said still feeling nauseous.

"Are you ok?" she looked at me like she was examining my x-rays.

"Yes, ma'am. I'm good, just tired," I lied.

"I'll be in there shortly, and I am so happy you came to see me, baby," she said, hugging me.

Leaving her arms and going to my mother's house was like leaving a warm fireplace and jumping into a tub filled with ice cubes. As I entered through the garage, I heard her and Maurice talking in the kitchen. I was not in the mood for any foolishness, but I knew I had to speak.

"Hey," I said, speaking to them and caring less if Maurice responded, which he didn't.

"Good afternoon," Mother replied. "So nice of you to join us."

"I've been here for about an hour," I said, feeling the need to defend myself.

"Oh, I know. That's why I said it is so nice of you to join us," she replied, pointing at herself and Maurice.

"Speak for yourself," Maurice said, looking away with his arms crossed like a little girl.

"I thought the whole purpose of this visit was to see Mama," I said, being blunt like Mama.

"Last time I checked, this is my house, and you don't come up in my house and not speak to me first," she said in all of her haughtiness.

"Wow, really Mother? I don't have time for this," I said, getting ready to leave but walking into Mama.

"What is going on in here?" Mama inquired looking at my mother.

"I'm telling your granddaughter whose house she is in and she shouldn't take so long to speak to me," Mother said, folding her arms and pouting like Maurice.

They were so similar, both spoiled brats.

"I'm sure she knows whose house this is. I wanted some alone time with her. Is that ok, Justine, that I spend alone time with my granddaughter?" Mama asked, using one of her trademark rhetorical questions.

"Yes, Ma'am," Mother replied like a scolded child.

"What is that smell?" I asked, and before I knew it, I made it to the trash can and vomited.

"Fatima, are you okay?" my mother asked still sitting next to Maurice.

"Come here, baby. Sit down. Maurice, get me a damp, cool washcloth. Justine, give me a glass of Ginger Ale," Mama said.

If it wasn't for her I would have been SOL.

"Here," my mother said, handing me a glass of Ginger Ale. "I'm glad you made it to the trash can and not on my floors. I just had the floors done."

"Justine, what are you smoking? Your daughter threw up, and you're worried about some damn floors. Hush the noise now," she said.

"Here, Mama," Maurice said, handing her the washcloth.

"What's wrong, Fatima? You've been looking a little peaked today," she said with loving eyes. She knew me all too well.

"I'm ok, just got a little bug," I said, feeling awkward, knowing my baby wasn't a bug.

"The same choices yield the same results, and that applies to us all," she said, rubbing my face.

I felt like a spear went into my side.

"Preach," Maurice said with a tone of condescension. *Did he just go there?*

"Touché! It's like wanting money and never getting a job," I snapped. We hadn't spoken at all and then he had the nerve to get in my business.

"I've got money. These jeans cost $200," he bragged.

"And where do you live again?" I fired back.

"Fatima, your brother is doing well with his guy group. I saw the making of their new music video," my mother interjected, always siding with him.

"And how much money did he hit you up for, Mother?" I asked now looking at her with disgust.

"That's none of your business, bitch," Maurice yelled with no constraint.

"Maurice!" Mama yelled.

"Bitch? Are you serious right now?" I looked at him and then my mother.

"Maurice, that wasn't nice, say sorry," she said as if he bumped into a stranger at a store.

"That's it? Say you're sorry. Really Mother?" I asked. "Well, at least this bitch doesn't pack peanut butter and spread jelly," I laughed.

"What does that mean, Fatima? I've never heard of that before," my mother inquired completely ignorant.

"Don't Fatima!" Mama begged shaking her head side to side.

I looked at her face full of love and decided to retreat. As I walked away almost reaching the stairs, he said it loud enough for me to hear.

"She probably had another abortion," he said loud.

"How much dick did you take or suck to get those jeans, Maurice? Let's be honest about everything! Yes, I have had abortions, plural! Probably not as many dicks as you have…"

My mother put her hand over her mouth. My grandmother incessantly repeated," *don't do it, baby.*"

"Fatima…," my mother began.

"Mother, at least Fatima pays for her mistakes because she owns up to them. You may resent my honesty, but I thought you hated lying," I looked at her with resentment for her judgment.

"Well, I do but…," she began.

"Then hate Maurice for hiding the fact that he is a faggot. A broke, lazy-ass, gold-digging fag," I shouted.

Maurice jumped up with tears in his eyes aiming at me as if he was going to hit me, only to land with my fist in his right eye. He was knocked off balance, and then I grabbed a knife off the counter and jumped on him, one hand choking him and another with the knife pointing at his chest.

"Fatima Antoinette Crosby, give me that knife right now! I rebuke you, Satan, in the name of Jesus Christ!" my grandmother shouted.

"Let her do it, Mama, I would rather die than live like this," he said, crying and pushing himself against the knife.

"If I were your mother, I would have aborted you," I spewed venomously, retreating from his chest as a small drop of blood came through his shirt.

My mother was crying hysterically and came to Maurice who didn't want to be touched. I just wanted to leave, but Mama followed me to my car.

"Look at me when I'm talking to you! You have never disrespected me, and you will not start today," she said as she walked behind me.

I looked at her with pain and horror because of my words and actions.

"I love you," she said, sounding like an angel, but then she slapped me. "Don't you ever pull a knife on your brother again! He is my grandchild whether straight, gay, or confused! I don't care. I love him and you should too!"

I cried and looked at her in awe because she had never slapped me before.

"You can't be mad at the world because you are making bad decisions. Stop treating your body like a trash can. Your lack of self-control is going to overcast the brightness of your future. I want God's best for you Fatima, but you have to also," she said as she hugged me. She cried, and I cried.

I wanted to tell her I was pregnant and I was thinking about getting married, but I didn't. *Stop treating your body like a trash can* remained with me for many days. I couldn't shake the feeling of emptiness and uncertainty even when Giselle arrived at my house. Giselle was spending two days a week at my place as she commuted to New York for a summer internship. It was no big deal because I was working out of Atlanta fifty-percent of the time. I just had to get through her first whole week of being with me when all I wanted to do was be alone.

When she arrived, I was on the phone with my mother who was in denial of Maurice being gay and attacking me for my actions.

"Mother, Maurice is draining you financially, and on top of that, I think he's using," I vented.

"Using what Fatima? Since you seem to know everything about my son," she flared back.

"Using drugs!" I was so tired of her naivety.

"Oh no, he's not," she pouted like a child.

"And I guess he's not gay either? Goodbye Mother," I said, getting off the phone. Giselle stood with her mouth ajar.

"That punk is going to get his one day, if I don't do him in myself," I ranted.

"And my mother is so blind to him. It's like he works magic on her or something, like Gator from Jungle Fever. Here, Mama, I'll do a dance for you. Got some cash?" I began dancing and placing my hand out.

"Well, there's nothing you can do, Fatima. Every family has a black sheep. Take my sister, Aaliyah. She is night and day from Dara and me. She was supposed to be graduating this June, but instead, she will be in summer school. She flunked two classes, and the classes she didn't, she barely passed. Who almost fails gym? Ms. Thing said she didn't want to work up a sweat or mess up her hair. And forget college; she'll be lucky to get into a community college."

"Well, at least that's an option. Maurice has no interest in school, working, or moving out of my mother's house. All he wants to do is get high with his little boyfriends. I wish my father was still alive; he would have kicked him out on his skinny, little tail."

"Hey, regardless of how we feel about our siblings, we still have to love them. Blood is supposed to be thicker than water."

"Yeah, unless you're dealing with a blood-sucking leach. I am twenty-five years old and got my own shit. There is no excuse for why his twenty-one-year-old ass can't do likewise. He should be giving Mama money instead of getting money from her. But, she's to blame too. I can't stand a weak ass woman. She never had backbone even when it came to Daddy, his drinking or his women. And now, his dumb ass is dead from cirrhosis of the liver, and she doesn't have a backbone with this damn fool. He's either going to die from AIDS or a drug overdose. But hey, that's no sweat off of my back. People get just what they deserve. I think God made AIDS for faggies and junkies. They're immoral, and they deserve it."

"Heterosexuals contract AIDS too. That's just a little too brash; I can't see anyone deserving such a fate. I don't even like thinking about things like that," she added.

"Girl, you should. Every time I meet a man, I don't care how good he looks. I always ask myself if there is the possibility that the nigga might be a potential junkie or faggie."

"Well, I'm sure you would know if he was."

"Not nowadays, girl. Niggas got all kind of stuff with them. I know this girl that was dating a model slash R&B wannabe singer from Silver Spring. Well, that loser was bi-sexual and, as far as I'm concerned a faggot. He looked just like a real man, but he had a woman's desire, the dick. I can't and will never be able to get with that shit. I'll just die politically incorrect. Shit, being Black is politically incorrect."

"Yeah, but people can tell you're Black. A homosexual doesn't need or have to disclose that kind of information. Keep your mouth shut, keep people out of your business."

"Yeah, well a punk who keeps his mouth shut about his sexual preference needs to keep his dirty ass out of my bed."

"Well, that's a two-way story. Keep the legs closed, keep the drama away," she teased.

"Ah, there you go," I smiled for the first time since she arrived. "Girl, my hat goes off to you about that virginity thing. Really, I wish I could have kept mine that long, but I didn't. And, girl, once you get some good dick, it's like a drug. You've got to get some more. The only problem is the asshole it's normally attached to."

"Can't be all that bad. What about Marc? You two seem to have hit it off. Girl, you even met his parents at graduation."

"Yeah, Marc is a nice guy, don't get me wrong, but there's one thing," I sighed. "I did it. I have to blame myself."

"What? What did you do?"

"I threw it on him, girl. He's whipped. Marc is pussy whipped. The boy wants to take permanent residency up my ass. He loves this stuff so much," I painfully gloated. "His new name is "Fatima Crosby's pussy."

"Yuck! And that's bad?" she laughed.

"There are two types of men. Men who you can't find half the time, and men who you can't get rid of. It's like, can I please have the middle man?"

"Oh really? I've never noticed," she said.

"Well, of course, you haven't. Chris wasn't a damn man. He was just a boy who you sported like a new pair of shoes," I walked across the room psychoanalyzing her boyfriends. "Now John, he's a different story. He seems to put a monkey wrench into my little theory."

"Yep, cause I like the time we spend together, never too much and never too little," she gleamed. "John just seems to be all I could want in a man."

"That's refreshing! I really hope that shit lasts. I really do. They all start off as dreams come true and then end up as your worst nightmare." I began to think of the painful reality of Marc, Charles, and the others before them.

"Fatima, you are so dogmatic. It can't be all that bad, can it?"

"Yep!" I simply replied, knowing my truth.

"Then, why do you even bother dating men? Why don't you just stay by your lonesome?"

"Because of her," I pointed to my crotch. "Sometimes, she gets tired of sticky fingers and Mr. Dill Dough, but you wouldn't know anything about that, now would ya?"

"Can't say I do," she laughed in total awe of my gesture. "So, men are just good for sex, huh?"

"Girl, if I could eat or fuck my own pussy, believe you me, I would. Just like if men could suck their own dicks, I'm sure they would. All men would walk around with permanent crooks in their necks."

"Fatima, girl, you are wild! You are out of this world!"

"But honest, babe! You can always depend on me to be honest. I say what I mean and mean what I say. Bottom line. No questions asked. That's what's wrong with people. Always caring what other motherfuckers think about them. Not me. To hell with whoever doesn't like me. They can kiss my black ass," I pointed to my derrière.

"So hostile," she sighed. "Everyone cares to a certain extent what other people think. You cared about what those employers thought about you when you were interviewing."

"Yeah, because it's hard to be opinionated when you're broke," I laughed. "Broke people can't afford to have opinions. They should only spend their time getting money."

"Now, I agree with that. Money does provide you with a certain amount of power to influence people's opinions. Particularly, their opinions about you."

"Exactly, and that's why I like Madonna. Forget the fact that she's white. No one can be perfect. But, that bitch doesn't give a damn what anyone thinks about her, and that's how she has made her benjies. Because when it's all said and done, it is all about the Benjamins baby," I started doing the cabbage patch.

We talked for a little while longer, but my mind volleyed between Marc and pregnancy. What had I gotten myself into? What was my next move? I hated my life; it seemed like all of my decisions brought me to a dark tunnel where there was no bright light on the other side to guide me. I was everything that Maurice said I was; and Charles, Jasper, and Marc were all living proof. For a moment, while I was on Maurice, I wanted to turn that knife on myself to end it all. At this moment in life, I realized that I was the common denominator in all my failed relationships and poor decisions. My greatest asset in life remained only in my ability to excel in my career.

7 | Darkest Hour

My first week of work was rough, but I made it. I wasn't showing, but I was approaching eight weeks and feeling so scared. I didn't know what to expect next. I had never made it that far before. Marc called me multiple times a day checking on me. A couple of days we had either lunch or dinner together. Whenever we saw each other, he made a point of putting his hand on my stomach when he kissed me. He said he liked making contact with our baby.

Marc wanted me to spend the weekends with him in Maryland so he could wait on me hand and foot. He was excited about his signing bonus from the firm where he received his job offer. His client would be the federal government, which meant he would be local between DC and Maryland. He decided to lease a townhome in Howard County, Maryland which was the halfway point. He hinted at having a house built there where our children could have a backyard. When he said the words "our children," I froze. This was becoming too real.

"Baby, I missed you," Marc said, hugging me tightly.

"We see and talk to each other every day," I said, still trying to digest his newfound love for me.

"I missed lying next to you and waking up next to you," he said, holding my hand while walking me to his new Audi.

"I didn't sleep well. I threw up two more times before I went to bed," I said, getting ready to sit when I noticed a dozen of white roses.

"These are for you," he said, placing them in my hand and kissing my lips.

"Thanks. What's the occasion?" I asked extremely curious.

"Just because I love you. I love us," he said, pressing his hand against my stomach.

"Thanks," I said, getting into the car.

"By the way, here, I bought you a book about pregnancy, and there's a chapter on morning sickness and possible remedies," he shared, handing me the brand-new book with a ribbon on it.

Wow," I swallowed deeply. "I don't know what to say. Thank you, I guess."

On the ride to his place, I looked out the window as he talked about his week at work. He asked me questions about my internship, and although I didn't feel like regurgitating my work week, I tried to oblige him.

"Sometimes, when we are having group meetings, and I have a suggestion or a possible solution, they say things like, *Wow, Fatima that was good. I'm impressed*," I said, remembering the comments of my white colleagues. "When other people offer ideas, they don't make those remarks. It's like..."

"It's like good job, monkey, you do have a brain," he laughed.

"So, you get it. Does it happen to you?" I asked.

"Am I Black? We have to score harder, think harder, and work harder than our white counterparts," he said, knowing our common duality.

"I went to the fucking University of Virginia, and some of these crackers went to the University of Maine. What the hell is the University of Maine? I'd rather get a degree from Wal-Mart," I vented.

"You know the deal. Even at school, some of them looked at us like we didn't belong," he added.

"Touché, breathing Black while living in a white world," I said as we pulled up to his place.

"I love Black women and would never disgrace my mother by marrying someone insufficiently and inferiorly different," Marc said, reaching out for my hand.

"I would never marry outside of our race and especially not a white man," I said, thinking about how weird it would even be having sex with a white man, especially given what I heard about their small penises.

Marc's townhome had three levels and was furnished modestly. Since he was just leasing, he wasn't going to spend a lot of money furnishing it. On Saturday, we went looking at houses in Howard, Montgomery, and PG counties. The houses that we loved were in a failing school system, and the ones we could settle for were in snowfall areas. We didn't mind diversity, however, being the only Black family or number two wasn't going to cut it.

At times, I had to pinch myself. In my last year of grad school, I was pregnant and looking for houses with Jasper's friend who wanted to marry me. Was it a dream or nightmare? Some moments, Marc was everything I could want as a doting father for my children. At other times, I wondered how he would be as a husband. His phone went off throughout the day. Sometimes, he would answer and sometimes, he would not. At one point, he turned his cell off, which I found odd.

"Why are you turning your phone off?" I inquired, thinking it was female-related.

"Getting some crazy text messages from Lynelle about wanting more child support now that I am out of school," he said.

"Well, you're going to do that anyway, right?" I asked.

"No, I'm not increasing my support. I will give her additional money as she needs it, but I have another child on the way. We need to prepare for all that entails," he said.

"Madison has absolutely nothing to do with that. Furthermore, this was not planned, and I'm not broke," I added.

"True, true, and true. However, I'm not a deadbeat. Madison wants for nothing. Lynelle just has dollar signs in her eyes. Probably looking to buy more purses and shoes," he vented.

"Men trip me out with that shit. Women can buy their own shit; it does actually take money to raise a child, and quite a lot if you're going to do it properly," I retorted.

"Everyone doesn't have a silver spoon and doesn't need one, Fatima," he said, throwing shade at my privilege.

"Well, evidently you are making sure one of your children has a silver spoon, and the other one doesn't," I said, rolling my eyes and thinking how much of a jerk he could be.

"I'm sorry, baby," he said, kissing my hand. "I will talk to Lynelle at the appropriate time, which is not when I am house hunting with my future wife."

He kissed my forehead, and I acquiesced.

Late afternoon, we stopped by the mall to grab a bite to eat and do some shopping. Marc was trying to get his wardrobe together for work. Things I took for granted my home, car, clothes, and shoes were in high priority areas on Marc's goals' list. My parents bought me a 3-series BMW for my Sweet-16. My brownstone was paid off and paying the taxes was just as simple as writing a check. I owned purses and shoes that cost more than all of Marc's clothing. As we were shopping and I began pointing out ties that I thought looked nice, he often responded that they were beyond his budget. Then, there was one he really liked but refused to pay $200 for it. Since his birthday was the next weekend, I made a note to self that I would buy him that tie.

When we left the mall, we had light conversation. Still nagging me in the back of my mind was the texts between Lynelle and him. What was so bad that he had to turn off his phone? When Marc got into the shower, he powered his phone back on, and I took the liberty of checking his messages. He only had one message from Lynelle, which was telling him Madison had a cold, and he wouldn't be able to pick her up next weekend. While reading the message, I began to fume when there was no mention of her wanting to increase child support. What was more interesting was about 20 texts from Rachel, which ranged from pictures of her modeling swimsuits at the store, and her stating incessantly that she misses him and hopes that we are having a good weekend together.

When I heard him turn the water off, I got off the phone. When he came out, I was looking at my phone. He asked what I was doing, and I said going through my text messages. I allowed him to dote on me the rest of the evening, but I barely slept. When he began to snore, I took his phone and went into the bathroom. Instead of looking at his texts, I went to Facebook and saw he had a notification in his inbox. I clicked Messenger to search his messages. His most recent messages were from Rachel. As I scrolled down, I saw that Marc had sex with Rachel the week we had that argument about her. I saw her inquiries about our relationship. His acting like a victim of a girlfriend he could never please. Then, I saw the pictures they sent to each other even after we made up. One picture he sent to me of himself posing in the bathroom with his shirt off and one hand down his pants. He had sent it to her first. She replied she would like to lick what his hand was holding. I wanted to throw up. I remember when he sent it to me and I replied *nice*. He said he didn't normally send pictures of himself to girls. What a liar! Every so often, Rachel would complain about her relationships and then say she wished she had someone like him. She also said she hoped I appreciated the king I had. She had given me a nickname, *Silver Spoon*. When it appeared he and I were having troubles, he would tell her his *Silver Spoon* issues.

Rachel2Hot2Hold: Hey handsome. I miss you. How's everything?

Me: Silver Spoon issues…SMH

Rachel2Hot2Hold: OMG, she's such a damn drama queen. What is it now?

Me: She's complaining talking about I'm being secretive. Like I'm hiding something.

Rachel2Hot2Hold: Silver Spoon got Red Bottoms, LV, and BMW and still insecure. SMHRH. She needs to be glad to have a king like you.

Me: I think she would prefer a servant LOL

Rachel2Hot2Hold: She needs to be serving you. I know I would.

Me: You're funny LMAO

Rachel2Hot2Hold: IJS, let's hook up soon. Want to show you my new tat.

Me: Where did you get it?

Rachel2Hot2Hold: Your favorite place ☺

Me: I can see you in 10 minutes

I was appalled beyond belief. When I cross-referenced the date of their messages with my text messages, it was the day I was sick, and he said he was too busy to come by to see me. It appeared once I got pregnant, he stopped communicating with her because she kept sending him messages just to say something.

When a man seems like he's too good to be true, he is too good to be true. That was the day I felt a darkness capture my soul. Some say revenge is best served cold, but the coldness would not come from his death but the death of my heart. I had to make Marc feel the pain I felt from his betrayal. I became consumed by an ominous yen to make him suffer and think twice before he did this bullshit to another woman. I had the ultimate plan to control-alt-delete Marc's ass out of my life with no rebuttal. When he took me home, he said next weekend would be very special so be sure to pack something nice. I knew he was going to propose to me.

All week, Marc was on cloud nine floating about the exosphere, while I plotted how to bury him in the Earth's core. I did some shopping because I needed our special night to be one he would never forget. I told him I would have to meet him at the restaurant because I got tied up at work and was running behind. When I arrived, he sat patiently at a table with red roses on it.

"Oh my God! You look so beautiful, baby! Red is your color!" Marc said, hugging me and pulling out my chair.

"Thank you. You look nice as well," I said with slight discomfort and pain.

"Are you two ok?" he asked as the concerned father-to-be.

"Oh, we're better than ever," I replied, grabbing my menu.

"Can I take your drink orders?" the waiter asked.

"I would like vodka and tonic, and water is fine for the lady for now," Marc answered so confidently.

"I'll have a white Zinfandel," I looked at the waiter.

"Babe, are you sure?" Marc asked, looking shocked.

"Yes, the baby won't be an alcoholic," I said as I began to peruse the menu.

"Babe, are you ok?" he asked but this time putting his hand on mine.

"I'm fine, just tired," I sighed as I retracted my hand from his grasp.

"Ok, we don't have to stay. I just wanted to switch up the scenery. But, the most important thing is you, me, and our baby. When we first met, I never knew I would be saying those words, but I am and Fatima it feels good. In fact, it sounds great," he said, getting down on one knee and taking a small box out of his blazer.

"Fatima, I didn't really give marriage strong consideration. I felt like when I had Madison, I had a strike against me. When we met, I didn't know you would become the love of my life."

As he spoke those words, my mind raced with images of all the times Rachel hugged him and the Facebook messages. I began to see images of them having sex. I missed some parts of his speech as my mind went into overload.

"Fatima, will you marry me?"

I said nothing as tears flooded my cheeks. He was happy and proceeded to put the ring on my finger. He took a napkin and wiped my tears.

"Oh baby, don't cry?" he said, kissing my nonresponsive lips.

"I'll be okay," I said, reaching into my purse and grabbing a long slender rectangular box nicely adorned with silver wrapping paper.

"Marc, I have something for you too. I would be remiss if I didn't take this opportunity to celebrate your birthday," I said, handing him the box.

"Wow, you are amazing! I thought you forgot when I didn't hear from you all day," he said, examining the box.

"Is this a little silver spoon?" he asked as he unwrapped the bow.

"Yes, you know how we like silver spoons," I said, thinking about my nickname.

"Is this that necktie? Oh my God, you shouldn't have," he said, removing the tissue paper. "Whoa, what is this?"

Before his eyes were two sonogram pictures.

"What are these?" he smiled.

"Wait a minute. This one right here is the picture the doctor gave us. But what is this one? There's nothing there? Fatima, what is going on, babe?"

"Look under the tissue paper," I replied.

As he lifted the tissue, he noticed the padding beneath them and when he turned it over, it was full of blood. He dropped it to the ground.

"What the fuck is that?" he yelled.

The wait staff rushed over to us.

"Marc, that is the picture I had taken this morning before I aborted our baby," I said devoid of emotion and looking in his eyes.

The look on his face was indescribable.

"Oh no, what have you done…," he cried in horror.

"I know about you and Rachel. I know everything. I saw your text messages and Facebook account. The next time you decide to fuck around with someone, remember the blood of your baby," I said, standing and grabbing my purse.

"What! Are you fucking kidding me? I don't love that girl! I didn't have sex with that girl," he cried.

"So, you killed our baby over some Facebook shit," he yelled. "From time to time Ken or Ray use my Facebook account."

"Oh, right and I am sure Casper the friendly Ghost does too! Do you know how unbelievable you sound right now?"

"You fucking whore! You've probably been fucking Charles, the great love of your life, the whole time," he screamed and stood up in my face as if he was going to punch me.

The restaurant staff tried to intervene.

"You are such a child. So, I get it now; you thought I was fucking Charles, so you fucked Rachel. The only problem is I wasn't fucking Charles and what you did with Rachel didn't just happen; that is something that you wanted. Tell Rachel, Silverspoon sends her best," I said, leaving.

"I hate you, you fucking bitch," he yelled, throwing a glass my way that missed me by inches.

Just wanting something to be over doesn't end it. I found myself once again being a repeat offender of a DAN (dumb-ass-nigga). Marc was my breaking point. I felt an evil touch my soul, and it was dark. I believe there is a dark place inside of everyone, a point of no return. On the exterior, I have always appeared to be immune to others' thoughts and opinions, but in some instances, I was just masking some level of insecurity or pain. This pain was familiar yet new. I actually entertained being married to Marc and having his baby which was my major offense to his infidelity. We had an argument and didn't speak for two weeks, and he screwed his "sister." He used our argument as an excuse to screw her, but the chemistry they had existed before and during our relationship. I had been honest with him about my past and present, but he did not reciprocate. I would rather be Charles' mistress than Marc's wife.

However, neither had any value. I wanted a love that was true and my own, but that seemed to only happen to others like Giselle.

"Hi, Fatima. Can I come in? I need to speak to you," she said, knocking on my bedroom door.

"Yeah! Sure! Come in. It's open," I said as if I was asleep. I wasn't really in the mood for small talk.

"Are you sleeping already? You don't have a hot date?" she inquired.

"Nope," I said, sitting up in my bed. "A man is the last thing on my mind right now!"

"What happened to Marc?"

"Marc, oh please. He is history, with a capital H.'"

"History?"

"Yes, as in the past, finito, finished…and quite frankly I'm not in the mood to discuss it right now. So, what's up? What do I owe the pleasure for this tête-à-tête?" I was highly irritated, and Giselle had a way of being passive-aggressive.

"If you're not feeling well, I can come back some other time," she said, trying to avoid what was on her mind.

"Giselle, what's up with you? What's on your mind? You're not good at avoiding conversations. You have never been. This is Fatima now."

"You're right. So here goes, Fatima. Before you introduced me to John, were you interested in him?"

"You're damn skippy I was," I nodded and smiled while reminiscing. "Every girl on campus was interested in him before you snagged him up," I added nonchalantly. I still wasn't in the mood for small talk.

"Well, did you make your interest known to him?"

"Did I?" I smirked then I stopped as I saw the troubled expression on her face. "Wait a minute…where is this examination coming from?"

"Well, John told me…"

"I see. John wanted to have sex, and when you wouldn't give him any, he threw the fact that I wanted him in your face to make you jealous. That's the oldest trick in the book. A good one, but an old one. Boys will be boys."

"I wish…"

"You wish? What happened, Giselle? You're not making sense. Earth to Giselle," I said, tapping on her head.

"I wanted to have sex with him, and he rejected me. He said it wasn't all about sex with me. That he wanted something more with me, and if he simply wanted some ass, he could have gotten some from you. That you practically threw yourself on him."

"Well, at least he's honest. I'll give that pretty bastard that much. But, why was it necessary for you to ask me? What part of it didn't you believe?"

"That my friend would hook me up with someone she wanted! Set me up with someone she threw herself on. That makes me feel like our friendship is some big joke to you!"

"Giselle, come on girl! Gimme a break! Do you think that I wasn't hurt when John rejected me? And then, he had the audacity to ask me about you? Do you think it was easy for me to think about my friend's potential happiness over my own?"

"Well…But…You didn't have to introduce us at all."

"Giselle, who are you fooling? Not me. Not John. Evidently, you're only fooling yourself. You wanted to meet John as much as he wanted to meet you. Don't play games. Plus, look at what you two have now."

"And what is that? A man that doesn't want to make love to me?"

"Well, at least he's not the typical brotha who treats you like you are the world so he can get some ass, and then months later have your ass up on the snatch man's table."

"What are you talking about? What snatch man's table? Fatima, you didn't…"

"Yes, Giselle. I had another abortion. I was pregnant by Marc, and I had an abortion. Not only didn't he give me any money, but he didn't even have the nerve to come with me to get the shit done," I lied, trying to end the conversation.

Perfect as planned. She stopped talking and looked at me with pity. She came toward me to hug me, but I told her I was good. Although I wasn't good, I didn't want her sympathy. I didn't want the comfort of a hug. I needed the pain to last to remind me never to get myself into this situation again.

8 | Recap

My summer flowed right into my last year of grad school. Everything in my life was a canvas of gray. The only hues of excitement were borrowed from Giselle's life. She and John finally had sex when he took her to an island getaway. Then, he threw her a surprise 25th birthday party surrounded by her family and friends. However, no matter how lovely the script of their romance played out, Giselle's skepticism of John could not be put to rest.

"Giselle, maybe the guy is really busy. It sounds like someone is spoiled to me. Why would he lie to you?" I asked.

Giselle was upset she couldn't see John for Christmas.

"I don't know. Another woman maybe?" she muttered under her breath.

"Ya think? John just doesn't seem like that type. It took him forever to go there with you. And now all of a sudden you think he's chasing skirts. Naw Gee, you've gotta come a lil' better than that."

"Hey, but he's there, and I'm here…and not seeing me for Christmas is just a little too much."

"So, what are you going to do, Giselle?" I asked with suspicion.

"I'm flying up there tomorrow after my last exam."

"Does he know this?" I already knew the answer.

"No, I'm his girlfriend. Why should I have to tell him? He came down here and surprised me for my birthday."

"Wow, girl, you've got it bad!"

"What?"

"You're whipped. And now you're going through withdrawal. It happens even to the best of us. I knew that nigga looked like he had some good stuff...Look at you...you're feigning," I tried joking to shake her seriousness.

"Whatever! Since he won't be able to visit me, I decided to visit him. What's wrong with that?"

"Sounds like someone is insecure to me. There's nothing wrong with you going to see your man but your motives are a little off to me...It's like you're looking for something to start some shit over. Relationships have enough shit with them. You don't need to go looking for it," I said, remembering Marc's Facebook.

"Well, first of all, I'm not insecure! I just believe if there's nothing to it, and if he's as busy as he says he is, then there won't be anything to find."

"Okay, got a question for you. What if he's working, how will you get into his place? What are you going to do? Roam the streets of New York City?"

"Aha," she said, pulling out a key. "He gave me a spare key to his place."

"Aw hell, why did he do that?" I shook my head.

"He probably thought I would never use it, but he guessed wrong. And like I said, if there's nothing fishy going on, then everything will be fine."

"For your sake, I hope everything is fine. But, Giselle, let me just leave you with this. Sometimes, when we go looking for a villain, we end up right where we started, looking at ourselves in the mirror. Believe me, I know." That was the recap of my year and life in general.

"Fatima, I love John with all my heart. But, I feel like something is wrong. I just have a gut feeling. I can't explain it."

"Well, girl, do whatcha gotta do. I just hope you don't end up regretting it."

"Me too. I really want the happily ever after with John. And if it's meant to be, then it will be."

That one decision changed the entire landscape of their relationship like my one decision. Giselle ended it with John because he lied about having a child. The whole story was quite confusing to digest, but the bottom line was he kept what she labeled a "big secret." Experience taught me that there is no variance in sizes of secrets. Secrets kill trust and shatter dreams.

The glimpses of brightness in my life came from the fact that I was graduating from college and starting my new career as a management consultant. I was offered a permanent job at the consulting company I did my internship with in Atlanta. My starting salary was $135,000 plus bonuses. Although the company's headquarter was in Atlanta, I could live anywhere because I had to travel to clients. I didn't mind the travel because it gave me a break from the monotony.

Graduation day was uneventful; both sides of my family came. Maurice was cordial and on his best behavior. Mama looked radiant and even more proud of me than my mother. In a fleeting thought, I wished my father was there. It was an awkward feeling. After my ordeal with Marc, a part of me was different. I had no interest in dating and just wanted to focus on my career.

With two months to spare before I started a new gig, I was to attend my sorority's annual convention. Normally, I served on the planning committee, however with finishing school and trying to get acclimated to my new job, I declined helping. I really just wanted to chill and keep things light and easy. Giselle asked if she could ride with me, which I didn't mind.

When we arrived at the convention, I knew most of the people there given that I was our chapter's president for two years. I attended all of the conferences and conventions and was able to get superb seating for the opening luncheon. Shortly after we sat, one of my line sisters, Nia, arrived.

"I'm glad I wasn't too late!" Nia said half out of breath.

"You haven't missed a thing," Giselle replied.

"I could miss everything but Dr. Lovejoy. I need to hear a word from her now," Nia said teary eyed.

"What's wrong, Nia?" Giselle said, patting her on the back.

I already knew it was her whorish boyfriend Fred, the NFL reject.

"Let me guess. Could it be Fred?" I said, being annoyed by the whole scene. "You need to leave him alone!"

"Fatima!" Giselle growled at me with piercing eyes.

"No, it's okay," Nia whimpered. "She's right. I just love him so much."

"Seems like you don't love yourself enough," I said, remembering Charles and Marc.

"Fatima, get a grip. All of us have made fools of ourselves in the name of love," Giselle vented.

"Alrighty then! We are definitely in the house. Wassup girls?" Khia exclaimed. She was a soror who graduated from our school two years before us.

"Hey, Khia! Wassup girl? You look fly. Almost as good as me!" I said, hugging Khia.

"Hi, Khia. How are you? Long time no see," Giselle added.

"Well, I just got back from London. My job sent me there for six months. It was an awesome experience. Those European men just love Black women. And the shopping was incredible!"

"Oh, by the way...did I tell you that I was engaged?" Khia said, aiming her ring directly at all of our faces.

"Wow, that is gorgeous! How many carats?" Nia asked with starry eyes.

"Like I would deal with anything under five, girl! And it's set in platinum!" Khia gleamed.

"What the hell is platinum but glorified silver? That shit has always been overrated to me," I added not really caring what anyone thought.

"Well, one day when or if you ever arrive in the upper echelon of life, sweetie, you'll know platinum is as far from silver as a diamond from zirconia," Khia answered with a smug look. "But then again, we shouldn't even be having this conversation; I'm the only one at this table who is engaged. Aren't I?"

"Last time I checked, you were also the only honky -dory-I've-gotta-marry-a-white-man-because-a-Black-man-wouldn't-put-up-with-my-snooty-ass...," I flared back, but Giselle interrupted me.

"I wish you the best Khia...and it is a nice ring," Giselle said, being Mother Teresa.

"I could have any man I want Fatima; my heart chose Brandon. But then again, what do you know about a heart? We Black women are always pigeon-holing ourselves. We can date and marry whoever we choose. And for your information, he is Columbian, not white."

"Well, anyone who is not Black might as well be white to me," I rebutted.

"Well, that's just like calling all people of color Black, Africans, or Jamaicans. People have other heritages of which they are very proud," Khia said, wasting her words.

"Well let me tell you something, you can do whatever the hell you want to do. When you marry outside of your race, it's like you're dissing your own people. When Black men marry outside, they might as well be saying their moms weren't good enough role models. So, they disrespect them by marrying other women, and the same applies to Black women. It's like your father wasn't crap, so your payback to him is marrying the other man," I answered to her babblings.

"Did you read this in a book or are these your own twisted delusions or fears that keep you in your cell of racial divide?" Khia vented.

"If Black people keep giving away their chromosomes, our damn race will become extinct, and what the hell is wrong with trying to preserve a beautiful race of people?" I asked, cutting right to the chase.

"I can't believe how ignorant you....," Khia began, but Giselle interrupted her.

"Ladies, please just agree to disagree because our food is coming and Dr. Lovejoy is about to come on," Giselle said, putting rest to the banter.

Dr. Vivian Lovejoy was a renowned soror and the conference's keynote speaker. She was labeled the relationship guru and love expert in several magazines. She also wrote books like *Love Rules: The Woman's Guide to Loving Herself.* I bought it but didn't read it; what I was looking for, I doubted it would be in a book.

"Some people ask me, Dr. Lovejoy, why aren't you married? And I tell them because I choose not to be. You can never have a fulfilling life living for others, their expectations for you and your life. Yes, I am an attractive Black woman from the inside out, and I would love to be married and have children. However, my life is the one thing that God gave me that is inherently mine, and I have to spend it wisely and to the fullest. I make decisions according to what is good for Vivian. So many

times, we find ourselves doing what another person defines as good for us but more so for them. Don't get trapped in that because people are fickle. People change. We all do. What was good to you five years ago or even yesterday might not be good for you today. Allow yourself room to grow, because with growth comes change. Don't put unreasonable expectations or timetables on yourself or others. Allow yourself to experience life and don't punish yourself for mistakes. Learn from your mistakes and share your experiences with others so you can release the agony, pain or disappointment from that situation. And in doing so, share a testimony with someone else of how life goes on. No situation, circumstance or person can stop life from going on. Life is a revolving door of people, situations, and circumstances. Learn to spend your time wisely. When we are born, I believe just like God has the hairs on our head's numbered, so are the days of our lives. What would you do differently today if you knew your last day was tomorrow? Use that as your guide for how to spend every day. You'll never know which moment is your last. One day, I was at a restaurant in DC eating by myself, and a waiter came up to me and asked, "Why are you eating alone, Dr. Lovejoy? You are too pretty to eat alone." As if a person who might not look as attractive should eat alone (she laughs). How many people like eating alone by a show of hands? Not many! I would rather eat alone in contentment than eat with company in misery. Don't keep company to avoid being lonely because you will find yourself keeping company with people who make you miserable. Associate with people because you enjoy being with them; they add something to your life and vice-versa. Don't find yourself in one-sided relationships where only one party is truly benefiting from the situation. There is always a price to pay, whether it's time, money or effort. Every minute you settle for less is sixty seconds of more you're missing out on. Once you discover you're not in a fulfilling relationship, resign yourself from it. Why prolong the inevitable? Are you not worth the very best? Not just some of the time but all of the time. On the other hand, don't believe in perfect people, they don't exist. Unless the reflection in your mirror is perfect, the person across from you can't be more than what you are. Don't put people on pedestals higher than you; you will always be unhappy with your findings. The only statement that a person can whole-heartedly live up to without fault or failure is I'm not perfect. When people tell you I'm only human, what they are saying is I'm not perfect, or rather I'm just like you. How many people in here by a show of hands have been disappointed by someone?"

Everyone lifted their hands.

"Now by a show of hands, how many people have let someone down? If there is anyone in here with her hand down, you need to set up your next appointment as soon as possible because we have all been there. We all have let someone down, whether our parents, a friend or ourselves."

At that moment, I began to think about all the poor decisions and choices I had made. More than anyone, I had let myself down, which became a rerun in my mind the rest of the conference and as I drove Giselle home. The conference, which I used to get so amped about, left me feeling empty. I felt like I was drowning in an endless sea of emotional females, and I was completely stoic. I needed a reprieve and was so glad Giselle, Nia, Cynthia (one of Nia's friends) and I were going on a girl's trip to Cancun. I needed to escape my normal, but before I left, my mother wanted me to meet her for dinner.

"Hello, Mother," I said, going directly to my seat.

She stood as if I was going to hug her and sat down just as quickly.

"How are you? I miss talking to you," she said, looking at the menu.

"I'm well. Looking forward to starting my job," I said, looking through my text messages.

"What are you doing this summer for fun?" she asked, but now looking at me.

"I'm actually going to Mexico tomorrow with some of my girls," I replied, looking at her. Something about her looked different.

"Mother, what's going on? We really haven't been talking since the Maurice incident," I said, trying to cut to the chase.

"I know you don't have the highest regard for me," she began.

"Hold up. I think it's the inverse," I rebutted.

"Let me talk, and then you can have your say," she insisted.

"Sure, why not, dinner is on you," I said, looking down at my phone again.

"Look at me when I am talking to you. Show me some respect, Fatima. I am your mother," she vented.

"Touché," I replied.

"Why do you hate me so much?" she whined.

"For reasons like this. Why are you doing this? A lot of things have been done and said over the years; I am fine with it, and you should be also," I replied, feeling myself becoming vexed.

"Fatima, stop judging me! You can't possibly know the road I have walked, the pain, the struggle, and regret.," she said with tears in her eyes.

"Are you serious right now? You are an elitist socialite; please miss me with the Harriet Tubman journey, Mother," I said, rolling my eyes. "If this is all, I will take a raincheck on dinner," I said, getting up.

"Sit down now!" she screamed. "It's time we have a talk, and that's what we are going to do, and you're not going to embarrass me any further in this damn restaurant. Do you hear me?" she demanded with glaring eyes.

"Yes, Ma'am," I said, returning to my seat in disbelief. She had never spoken to me like that.

"Sorry for yelling at you, but Fatima, like it or not, I am your mother. I don't know where I went wrong with you or us. Why do you hate me so much?' she asked, looking directly into my eyes.

"I don't hate you," I replied.

"Ok, why don't you like me?" she continued.

"Why don't you like me?" I rebutted.

"I love you, Fatima. I may not like some of your actions or decisions, but I do love you," she insisted.

"I didn't know the conversation changed to love; thought we were talking about like. I am the summation of my decisions and actions. Therefore you don't like me. But guess what, Mother? I'm fine with that. You don't like me, and I don't respect you," I retorted.

"So, there we have it. Why don't you respect me?" she asked.

"I really don't want to do this with you," I said, trying to escape the inevitable. I didn't respect her, but I wasn't trying to hurt her.

"I'm a grown ass woman, birthed two children, miscarried two, and now a widow. I think I can survive your answer," she said, shocking me about the two miscarriages.

"What's wrong? You look shocked," she said, looking at me. "Didn't know I had two miscarriages? There's a lot you don't know about me. But, let's not get side-tracked. Why doesn't my only daughter respect me?" she continued.

"Because you don't respect you!" I finally let it out. "You married a man for money and let him walk over you until the day he died. What is respectable about that?" I said, releasing my years of disappointment thinking my mother was a doormat.

"So, you believe that I am some gold-digging victim of your father's? Is that right?" she asked almost smiling.

"Basically," I said, hoping the conversation would end.

"First of all, I don't recall meeting many gold-diggers in medical school. Fatima, you know that I do not come from average means. So, your father could not do anything for me that I couldn't do for myself," she began.

"But, you gave up being a doctor and then had to live off him," I interrupted.

"My naïve daughter, one day when you get married you, will learn there is no mine or his, it's ours," she smiled as if I told a funny joke.

"Anyway, I met your father through a medical student I was dating, Peter Amos," she said, causing my jaw to drop.

Peter Amos was my first love's father. Why did I not know about this?

"Yes, Mr. Peter and I were an item," she said, responding to my astonishment.

"I never knew that. What happened?" I asked, wondering how she went from one friend to the next.

"Peter, who was two years ahead of me like your father, was idealistic and wanted to save the world. He came from humble beginnings and felt like it was his life's mission to help others. My parents paid too much money for me to travel the world doing mission work in other countries. So, when he graduated, we tried to make it work, but it didn't. Toward the end, your father came at me strong. We found out that we had common interests and similar upbringings," she said, reliving the details in her eyes.

"Once your dad finished his residency, he asked me to marry him, and I said yes. However, I delayed getting married until I finished the last years of my residency. During that time period, I had begun hearing some things about him being a ladies' man. However, I ignored them because I thought it impossible for him to have time to do anything but work and spend time with me," she said with a blank look.

"So, when did you find out he was a whore?" I asked, cutting to the chase.

"A week before we got married. He was working late one night at his office, and I surprised him with dinner. I saw him standing in his office with his back to me fully clothed, but he was making noises. When I said hello, he turned around, and his penis was out of his pants, and a woman was on her knees with semen dripping down her face," she said, shaking her head.

"What the hell! Are you serious? Why did you still marry him?" I asked.

"He swore it was the only time it had happened. She was a patient who he shouldn't have allowed himself to get close to, but when her husband cheated on her, she started confiding in him. He said she offered him head, and since I didn't do oral sex, he didn't think it was a big deal. I wanted so badly to believe him, and I didn't want to be embarrassed having to let everyone know that the perfect couple was marred," she said.

"Image meant more to you than trust and love?" I asked.

"When someone lets you down, Fatima, you don't automatically stop loving them although you might stop trusting them. Yes, in hindsight I guess image meant more," she answered.

"So then, once you discovered he wasn't going to change, why didn't you leave?"

"When we got married, he was perfect. Our life together began to thrive, and we had you. Peter moved back to DC, and he was married. We all decided to let bygones be bygones, and he and your dad opened their practice together. Shortly after, I was pregnant and miscarried after four months. The next year, we were pregnant again. Craig Jr. was going to be his namesake. However, I miscarried at six months," she said with a tear in her eyes.

"I am so sorry. I never knew this," I said, reaching for her hand, but she withdrew it.

"There's more. Your dad said the stress of me working was causing me to miscarry, so we decided I would come home. It was a rough patch in our lives. He started drinking and staying out late. Through counseling, I found out I was depressed. Some days, I didn't want to get out of the bed. I felt like less of a woman for losing two babies. That's when we hired our first nanny to help me with you. The morning of your third birthday, I left the house to pick up your cake but forgot my wallet. When I came back, I just parked in the driveway and came through the back-kitchen door. There they were; she was bent over, and he was pounding her like an animal. He kept slapping her butt and calling her a bitch. While I looked in awe, you came running in the kitchen, and I ran to you to cover your eyes," she said, reliving the painful memory.

"That was Linda the Mexican chick?" I inquired. "I wondered what happened to her. I don't remember any of it."

"Your dad moved out for about six months. I was contemplating divorcing him. During that time, Peter became my rock, everything I needed to make it through the hell I was experiencing. One weekend while you were with your dad, Peter came to see me. He and Priscilla were on the verge of getting a divorce likewise and somehow; we found comfort in one another. After that night, we swore it wouldn't happen again, but it did. However, Priscilla started threatening to take her life, and he didn't know what to do; he was scared she might try something crazy in front of Andrew, so we ended it. When your dad and I reconciled shortly after, I found out I was pregnant. I thought it was a sign from God that we were meant to be, that the heavens were finally shining down on us. However, my weeks did not correspond to our reconciliation. We had a choice to make. Craig felt like he owed me because of all his indiscretions," she said.

"So, Mr. Peter is Maurice's father?" I asked completely shocked.

"Yes," she replied simply.

"And Dad knew?" I asked.

"Yes," she said.

"Does Maurice know?" I asked.

"No," she said with tears in her eyes.

"Mr. Peter was fine with all of this?" I asked. "I just can't see him being fine with being an absentee father. He loved Andrew."

"He doesn't know," she said, breathing heavily.

"Mom, oh my God! You can't be serious. Y'all didn't tell him?" I asked in disbelief.

"That was the promise. Your dad's payback to Peter was for him to think we reconciled and had a baby," she said, looking devoid of feeling. "He just took it to the next level when he started fucking Priscilla."

"I feel numb right now. No wonder Maurice feels like Dad never cared for him. And I made it worse by saying he stayed away because of him," I said, regretting my words and actions toward Maurice.

"It's no one's fault. After Maurice, we tried to have another child only to find out your father had a low sperm count. He said he felt cursed. Something in him never rebounded, and he drank himself to death," she said, staring off.

As we sat in my car before we departed, I had to know why she decided to tell me all of her sordid past with my father. However, before I could ask her, she started crying, and for the first time in my life, I held my mother in my arms. She wept as if shackles had fallen off her soul. I dared not ruin the moment with my curiosity. However, she ended the moment by telling me that Priscilla died. She overdosed on cocaine and was found dead in the bathroom. She was attending the funeral next week and needed someone to go with her. Fortunately, I would return from Cancun the day before the funeral and agreed to go with her.

9 | Party Time

I couldn't sleep on the plane, unlike the girls. My mind raced with all my mother had shared with me. As soon as we got to the resort, we were greeted with cold-scented hand towels and cocktails. After we unpacked, we hit the beach. It felt good to breathe, different air. I didn't feel as suffocated as I did when I was at home in the US.

The Mexican men were all over us like we were burritos, tacos, and enchiladas. Although flattering, I was hardly interested. Men were off my radar and especially ones who needed a green card. Our first night we met a group of guys who all went to college together. Troy was Cape Verdean. Mike lived in Baltimore and was a government worker who seemed to have his eye on Giselle. Larry was the odd ball, a tall white southern-good-old-boy from Louisiana who looked like Matthew McConaughey. He was a technology attorney for a Fortune 100 based in Atlanta. Every night they would gravitate to us, which I didn't mind because they spoke English.

"You ladies look so nice," Mike said, sitting down next to Giselle.

"You don't look too bad yourself, Mike," I said, giving him the once over. "You don't really fit the part of a government worker."

"And what would that be?" he asked.

"Well, when I think of a government worker, I think of someone who dresses like it's still the 80s. Still rocking gear from Merry-Go-Round," I said, making everyone laugh.

"Why is that?" Giselle asked.

"Everybody knows the only real money a government worker makes is in overtime. Outside of that, that stupid pay grade scale they're on, it would take twenty years to start making some decent money," I said.

"Very insightful, Fatima," Mike said, seeming unwounded by my statements. "But there is no salary that can compensate for a person loving what they do every day. Every day, the experiences with my kids are more rewarding than taking some over-glorified high salaried job making just enough to impress the Joneses."

Well, excuse me Grade 10 level 2 is what I wanted to say, but I remained silent. I didn't want to banter with this guy with whom my best friend appeared to be smitten.

"Fatima, I know your husband must be so lonely without you," Larry said with his southern drawl.

"I guess he is...," I said abruptly.

"We're all single," Nia said, getting me back for the conference squabble.

"Oh, you are? I'm surprised darling," Larry drawled.

"Yes, I am," I said a little annoyed. "Why are you so surprised? What is it to you? You must be single yourself," I snapped.

"Excuse me if I offended you. I just thought that such a beautiful woman as yourself would not be single," he said, smiling.

"Heard that one before. That's crap! Why would you bother speaking to me if you thought I was married or something?" I insisted.

"Or were you thinking because I am Black you probably could get some quick action on the side. You know us Black folks, we don't have morals now do we?" I said, imitating his southern drawl.

"Well, I didn't see a wedding ring, so I stepped out on faith. The Bible says a man finds a wife; they usually don't just pop up in your mailbox saying "hi honey, I'm home," he said, making all of us laugh. But why the hell did he bring up *Bible* and *wife*?

"You being Black only makes you beautiful in my eyes. Not easy, but to the contrary, more challenging and interesting, Fatima," Larry said.

"Interesting and challenging like the damn naked African women your people exploit on National Geographic. To see your white women naked is art or pornography. To see our people naked is science, something worthy of discovery; something interesting, as you would say. Look, don't embark upon challenges you can't win. You know how you white boys are, when things don't turn out how you want, you go postal," I laughed but was still irritated. Why was he bothering me?

"First, I would like to preface your first statement that African women on National Geographic are there not for the exploitation of their bodies, but more so for the discovery of other people and cultures, it's not science but ethnography. Second of all, although all mankind began in Africa, you, my dear, are not African no more than me. I have been to Africa, and a lot of Africans don't exactly share these sentiments of mutual brotherhood or endearment some Black Americans seem to feel. Finally, you seem to know a lot about white men, but I take it that it's not from personal experience. You can't judge an entire race based off of your limited exposure, but then again you can do whatever you would like. But guess what?"

"What?" I snapped with a glaring eye of contempt.

"I still like you and think you are if not the most beautiful woman I have ever had the pleasure of meeting," he said, leaning into the table closer to me.

"Flattery gets you nowhere. Didn't your mother tell you that? Maybe compared to the southern belles or country club girls you're used to dating, I probably am different. Nonetheless, I don't know if you're qualified to judge Black beauty based on of your limited exposure. Anyone different might seem exotic or interesting," I said, trying to recompose myself.

"I have traveled most of the world, five out of seven continents to be exact, and have seen a cornucopia of women of all complexions, sizes, heights, and languages. So, believe me, I don't say this to flatter you. Flattery is a device used to edge around the truth while concealing a lie," he gleamed.

"Oh," was all I could muster as I gulped my drink.

"I keep telling you, partner, Black women are tough," Troy patted Larry on the back, while Larry kept staring at me.

"Why, because we aren't easy? And what the hell is a Cape Verdean anyway?" I directed my anger toward him.

"Fatima, you should have left that chip on your shoulder at home, this is a vacation. You're supposed to relax. Don't be so uptight. And this advice I give to you for free, being a government worker and all," Mike laughed.

"So, would you like to dance? I'm not a Michael Jackson, but then again, I'm not a Pee Wee Herman either," Larry insisted.

"White men can't jump, but now they can dance?" I said, lightening up the atmosphere.

"Well, I can't speak for all white men, but there's a lot I can do. But, for the time being, a dance would be nice," he smiled.

As I opened my mouth to reject his offer, Nia answered for me and helped me out of my seat. Shortly after that, Troy and Cynthia got up and danced. Then Mike asked Giselle and Nia to dance with him. It was okay, but I felt uncomfortable with how Larry was looking at me. It was like he was looking through me.

Later that day before we went down for dinner, I wanted to talk to Giselle. I was still bothered by Larry.

"The nerve of that redneck trying to put me on the spot like that," I vented.

"A southern gent, not a redneck, and I think he was cute," Giselle drawled, trying to lighten things up.

"I have to admit he wasn't bad on the eyes, but still...," I began.

"What? He's white! Come on, Fatima, this is the 21st century," she said.

"I don't see you dating one," I exclaimed.

"And? What's your point? If I met a man I was compatible with and found him physically attractive, I would date him regardless of his skin color. Well at least I would like to believe I would," Giselle rebutted.

"What if things got serious? Would you marry outside of your race? I mean, I have met some of the craziest biracial people, more than I would have ever cared to meet," I said.

"Fatima, that is a personal decision. Only you know what you can deal with. Larry seems like a nice guy, and you must have something for him, or we wouldn't be having this conversation," Giselle smiled.

"Well I mean, I'm not blind. Anyone can tell he is fine. Did you see his damn muscles? Girl. But hey, you know what they say about white men, and I can't be with someone who can't please me in bed."

"Who are they anyway? Who is actually going around measuring men's penises, Fatima? Do you hear yourself? You went from talking about him being a redneck to marriage, then kids and now sex. Get a grip, girl. You're scaring me."

"What the hell am I thinking anyway?" I huffed. "It wouldn't work anyway. We are too different. Did you hear him bring up a wife and the Bible? He's also a little on the conservative side, and I know he probably couldn't handle my ghetto ass. You know I have a strong attraction for thugs anyway. That's employed thugs mind you. Then in addition to that, I don't like long distance relationships."

"Fatima, what are you talking about? You will be working in Atlanta fifty percent of the time anyway. You told me on several occasions that you wouldn't mind moving down there. It seems like you are trying to rationalize yourself out of liking Larry."

"Am I that transparent?" I asked.

"Hey, Ms-Keep-It-Real, you need to take your own advice for once. You never know what might happen."

"I just got so much shit going on that at this point, I think a man would probably be more of a distraction than an enhancement."

"Then, just chill. You have been through a lot, and you still have to deal with your mother and Maurice when you get back home," she said, reminding me of what I was trying to escape.

The next morning, I couldn't sleep so I took a walk and went to the pool to lay out. Lo and behold, Larry was there swimming. He looked so fine in his swim trunks. There was no one else out there, so I had to speak although I just wanted to be alone.

"Good morning," I said, looking at him getting out the pool. Thank God, I was wearing shades.

"Good morning, Fatima. Are you going for a swim?" he asked.

"No, just came from a walk and wanted to chill by the pool," I said, hoping he would catch a hint.

"You have a lot going huh?" he asked.

"Huh? How did you deduce that?" I asked shocked at his accurate conclusion.

"You're up at 6am in Mexico. Doesn't sound like a vacation to me. Seems like your thoughts are keeping you awake," he analyzed me.

"Well, thank you, Dr. Phil," I laughed.

"I'm up for the same reasons," he said, looking away for the first time.

"What's going on in Mayberry?" I joked.

"I'm feeling like God is getting ready to move me in my career and I am feeling uncomfortable," he said.

"That's deep. And you know it's God?" I asked, puzzled how he could be certain.

"Once you've heard his voice you will know," he said, looking at me once again.

"I haven't heard his voice then," I said, trying to recollect my life in fleeting moments.

"Are you saved?' he asked.

"Saved from what?" I asked completely oblivious.

"From Hell," he laughed. "Have you accepted Jesus as your Lord and Savior? Are you a Christian?"

"Wow, let's unload some of that. I guess I am saved from Hell although most recently I feel like I am living it. I am a Christian, well kinda through my grandmother. I outsource my religious life to her. But, I don't go to church except for special occasions."

"It's all good. So, tell me about your grandmother, to whom you outsource your religious life," he said.

"I call her Mama. She's my everything. She just turned 72 in Dubai with her boyfriend. She lives in Texas," I said, remembering how great it felt to see her.

"Is this your paternal or maternal grandmother?" he asked fully engaged.

"My maternal grandmother," I answered.

"How is your relationship with your mother?" he asked.

"It's not the best but not the worse. Why do you ask?"

"You call your grandmother Mama," he said, smiling.

"Oh, Mother feels more like an older sister and Mama feels like a mother," I said, not believing I shared such intimate details about myself with a stranger.

"How does your mother feel about that?" he asked.

"That's one of the reasons why I'm up at 6 in the morning talking to a complete stranger," I joked.

"I'm sorry, don't want you to feel uncomfortable," he said.

"No, I'm good. I probably need to talk to someone who doesn't know me," I said, feeling relaxed.

We talked for another hour, and Larry did more asking and listening than anything else. For some odd reason, I felt at ease with him, so I began to unload. I figured what is said in Mexico will stay in Mexico. I shared an abridged version of my childhood, my family, and also about my experience with Marc. I told him what my mother shared with me about Maurice's father. He never interrupted me, just took it all in. Once I unloaded all my garbage, I asked what he thought.

"Fatima, hurt people hurt people," he said.

"Which people are you referring to?" I asked, not knowing whether it was my mother, my father, Marc, or me.

"Everyone you just shared. Your father was hurting. He married someone who really loved someone else but settled for him. To further that hurt, they kept miscarrying. Your mother was hurt because the man she wanted chose a cause over her. She rebounded with your father, and once he betrayed her, she felt rejected and was longing for love. She treated you more like a sister than a parent because she didn't want you to reject her too. Right now, given the death of Mr. Peter's wife, she's probably contemplating telling him the truth, and once again risking rejection. Your brother is hurting because, intrinsically, he felt rejected by your father and your mother didn't know how to parent. Today, she is still trying to buy his love because she feels guilty about the secret she kept."

"Whoa, that is some deep shit when you put it that way. So, what about Marc?" I asked, trying to see if he, too, was a hurt person.

"He thought having his daughter out of wedlock was a strike against and his parents probably reinforced that sentiment. Therefore, he wanted to prove to them he was not a loser. He goes to a top-tiered business school and then dates an upper-class model," he said, smiling at me with gentle eyes.

"A model? You're funny!" I laughed. "So, why did he fuck over me?"

"Hurt people hurt people. His ego was broken, and he looked externally to triage by being with girls who thought he was an A man while he felt like a C man with you. He felt like he was out of his league, which he probably was," he said.

"I felt such a darkness cover my soul, and the crazy part is I didn't even love him. I didn't want to marry him," I said, feeling tears coming to my eyes.

"So, how do you feel about what I did?" I asked not knowing how he would respond.

"The Bible says vengeance belongs to the Lord. We never win when we try to get even. Sometimes, when we shoot the shotgun of revenge, one barrel is pointing at the person, and the other barrel is pointing back at us. In the end, you only created an enemy. However, I have not a heaven or hell to put you in. You were a hurt person that responded in hurt," he said, putting his hand out for me.

"What are you doing?" I asked.

"Join me for breakfast. It's 8 o'clock," he said, looking at his watch.

"Are you serious? We talked that long! It doesn't feel like it," I said in awe.

"I'll take that as a compliment," he said, blushing.

"You should," I laughed. "I probably should get back to my room. The girls might be up by now. I'll see you around."

"I hope so," he said, still helping me up.

Larry was so fine. I wanted to kiss him, but instead, I hugged him and thanked him for listening to me. Once I reconnected with the girls, I couldn't stop thinking about Larry and the advice and counsel he gave me. I started thinking about what it would be like to date a white man. However, I felt uncomfortable entertaining the thought. Why was it bothering me so much? The more I saw Larry, the more my mind wondered what would be wrong with us maybe hanging out from time to time. He looked so fine and seemed to have some scruples about him. As our week ended and we all prepared to go our separate ways, Larry asked me for my phone number, and I gave it to him. Giselle almost died.

"Hey Fatima, this is Larry. I hope your flight home was uneventful yesterday. I'm back in the A preparing for work next week. Just wanted to see how you are doing. Call me when you can," Larry's voicemail message played. I accidentally left my phone at home when I went grocery

shopping. So, Mr. Larry Martin was thinking about little ole me. Why is he single? He's ten years my senior, no children, and no girlfriend. Why?

"Hello Larry, this is Fatima," I said a little nervous.

"I know your voice," he laughed. "Thanks for returning my call."

"No biggie. So, what's up?" I asked, cutting to the chase.

"Just wanted to say hi and see how your trip back home went," he drawled. It was adorable.

"Well, hi and it was uneventful. Anything else?" I asked.

"Nope, have a great evening," he said, shocking me.

"That's it? You were about to get off the phone?" I asked a little annoyed with how fast he gave up.

"There are 24 hours that God gives us every day. I like to use mine with purpose. I don't like people wasting my time, and I am respectful of others' time," he replied sternly. Oh, brother, he didn't have a sense of humor.

"Well, I was just kidding with you," I replied.

"Oh, I thought you were testing me to see if I would give up or beg you to stay on the phone with me," he said, reading right through me. How dare he!

"Larry, you called me. I'm not one for lectures," I snapped.

"How about this, Fatima, I am glad you made it home safely. Have a good evening. You have my number; use it at your discretion. God bless and good night," he said, ending the conversation.

"Goodnight," was all I could muster. Did he just handle me? Who does he think he is? Call him? He's out of his mind. So many thoughts flooded my mind. I didn't know if I was offended or intrigued. In either case, I decided to Google Larry Martin. There were news articles about him. I saw some of his Facebook and Twitter posts. He appeared to be active in nonprofits. I just kept scrolling and clicking for about an hour. For some reason unbeknownst to me, he had piqued my curiosity, but I was too stubborn to give in to it.

My mother called to remind me of Priscilla's funeral. When I picked her up, she was waiting at the door. She seemed very tense. I could only imagine how she felt seeing Mr. Peter after all this time. I asked why she didn't have Maurice join her. She said he had other plans, and she didn't want to bother him. I was kind of glad because it would have been awkward knowing that Mr. Peter was Maurice's father and Andrew was my brother's brother. It was completely crazy to me. The last time we saw them, I was 15 and Maurice was 11. I was apprehensive about seeing Andrew since the last image we shared together was of my father screwing his mother doggy-style.

The funeral was in Northern Virginia where they lived. There were about a couple hundred people there, mostly family. When we came around to greet the family, I instantly recognized Mr. Peter. He was as handsome as I remembered and looked distinguished reminding me of Denzel. Next to him was a chubby dude with a pretty, Asian girl. It was Andrew; he had gained a whole person in size and was married to a Korean girl who looked like she weighed 80 pounds.

During the funeral, I comforted my mother although I could not tell why she wept so hard. Her true relationship was with Mr. Peter, not Priscilla. I wondered how Mr. Peter would feel if he knew Maurice was his son. I wanted to ask my mother if was she was going to tell him, but I didn't want to push her. After the burial, we headed to the repast and she said she contemplated telling him the truth, but she didn't know how to do it. I told her she should invite him to lunch.

At the repast, they shared about 10 minutes, and she did as I suggested; and he agreed to do so in a couple of weeks. At that moment, I felt proud of her for taking a step in the right direction. On the ride back to her house, she thanked me for supporting her and not judging her too harshly. Larry's words came to mind, and I told her *hurt people hurt people,* and I cannot judge her for the pain she has had to endure. The moment ended with us hugging one another, and as she turned to wave goodbye, I said, "I'm sorry for rejecting you. I love you, Mom." She ran to me and embraced me hard as she cried, which made me cry.

With a new burgeoning relationship with my mother, I had a positive outlook on my life. I had a couple of weeks before I started work and wanted to prepare myself for the life of a consultant. I did a major cleaning of my closet, donating clothes and shoes to a women's shelter. I bought some new outfits for work and a journal. I read somewhere that highly successful people journal. I wanted to catalog my journey to success. So, I began my day writing my goals and ended the day writing my accomplishments.

The day before I flew to Atlanta to start my new job, I went to a small coffee shop downtown DC to journal in a different environment. When I got my coffee and went to sit at a table, I saw Charles. He was with a woman who seemed about his age. I tried to avoid eye contact with him, but no such luck. He excused himself from the table and called my name. I contemplated leaving the coffee shop, but he was too fast.

"Hi Fatima, long time," he said, pulling out the chair for me.

"Hi, Charles. Yes, a long time," I said, refusing to make eye contact.

"Let me see your beautiful eyes," he smiled, as he reached to touch my face. I politely dodged his hand.

"Don't leave your company waiting," I said, nodding to the woman who was engaged in her cell phone.

"Naria will be ok. She's a friend," he said, and for the first time, I noticed he did not have on a wedding ring.

"A lot has happened since last year. Can we do dinner tomorrow night?" he asked, looking boyishly shy.

"Sorry, I'm flying out to Atlanta tomorrow," I replied.

"Business or pleasure," he asked.

"My job," I replied trying to end the conversation.

"Perhaps another time. By the way, congratulations on your graduation. You have success written all over you," he winked as he walked away.

So, he was telling the truth. He did divorce his wife. Was his friend one of his patients? Whether married or single, Charles was not to be trusted. Of this, I was certain. Calling him or having dinner with him were definite noes. As I packed my suitcase that night, I ran across a souvenir group picture of our last night in Cancun. My eyes zoomed in on Larry. I was traveling to the A, as he would say. Calling him was a possibility.

10 | The Invention of Race

Waiting on a plane was just as bad as waiting for my period to come. Because I hadn't been sexually active for over a year, I stopped taking the pill, and now it seemed harder to predict when my menstrual would come. On the plane ride to Atlanta, I kept going to the bathroom to check and no *Mary*. I got my rental car and made it to my hotel near the airport. I had stayed there before during my internship, so it was almost like a second home. The bellhops remembered me and jumped to assist me with my luggage. In anticipation of my first day, I laid out my clothes and steamed them. I don't know why I had nervous energy. Before too long, I grabbed my phone and made a call.

"Hi Larry, this is Fatima," I said nervously given our last conversation.

"I know your voice," he said as he did before.

"I'm in Atlanta. I just got here a couple of hours ago. My first day of work is tomorrow," I said, trying to make sure he knew I wanted to talk.

"Great, hope you have a productive first day," he replied not seeming too entertained by me.

"Have you eaten dinner yet? I would like it if you would join me for dinner," I said as a lump entered my throat. What the hell was I doing? Did I just ask him out?

"No, I haven't, and I would love to have dinner with you," he replied, making my insides drop.

"Um, well there's a restaurant in my hotel if you don't mind coming here," I said, not knowing where else to suggest.

"Not a problem. I will shower and change. Is seven too late?" he asked.

"No, that will be great," I said, getting off the phone. I was nervous. I called Larry; he took me up on my offer, and now I was nervous. I was going to change my clothes, but why? This was going to be two buds having dinner. We weren't even friends yet; he was a stranger. I had to journal.

I am going to dinner with the guy I met in Cancun. The white guy, Larry. What am I doing going to dinner with a white guy in one of the Blackest cities in America? When did I begin caring what people thought? What am I doing? I shared so much dirty laundry with him in Mexico; he might look at me like a charity case. Why do I care? But he didn't judge me rather he tried to help me make sense out of my drama. He was kind and calm. Does he still think I'm attractive or did the awful truth about me make me less attractive? Why do I care?

I wrote as much as I could before I ripped the page out and threw it away. I made my way downstairs when he called and told me he was valeting. I freshened up a little before I went to greet Mr. Martin.

When I turned the corner, my eyes ogled this gorgeous man with strong cheek bones, a cleanly shaved face, and beautiful amber brown eyes. His hair was a blondish brown and well-groomed. He had such a sexy swagger about himself, which I should have known since two of his close friends were Black. When I reached in to hug him, his cologne held me hostage.

"Hey thanks for coming to have dinner with me. I hope this isn't too far from where you live," I said, feeling a little shy. I'm not shy. Why am I nervous?

"It's about 20 minutes. I live in Midtown," he said, pulling out my chair. The last time a man pulled out my chair was Charles at the coffee shop, and that was unwelcomed.

"You look as beautiful as I remember you," he smiled catching me off guard. He did still find me attractive.

"Thanks, you don't look too bad yourself. You've got a little swagger about yourself," I laughed. "I'm surprised you're single. Why are you single Larry?" I had asked before I knew it.

"Wow, we went from hi, compliment, to marital status," he laughed shaking his head. "I'm looking for my wife."

"Well don't you need to date so you can find out who she is," I asked, anticipating his answer.

"I have dated and will only do so again if I feel the woman might be the right one," he replied.

"Wow, so the next chick you date, you're going to marry? Who does that?" I asked unable to hold my laughter.

"A man who knows what he wants. A man that is led by God, that's who. Do you want to get married?" he asked once again, catching me off guard. Suddenly the air got thick.

"Uh, I don't fucking know. Marriage is scary," I said, thinking of my parents' marriage and even Charles' marriage.

"What's scary Fatima? Is it marriage or divorce? Which are you scared of?" he asked, looking through me. How did he know my thoughts?

"Shit, both! Hey, let's order something before this waitress comes back one more time with that simple look on her face," I said, grabbing my menu. Why was I so anxious?

We ordered our food and began small talk about our respective jobs. From what I could tell he was from money. My family did well, but his family was uber-wealthy. He seemed to love his family but expressed that they wanted him to marry a long time ago. He said unlike his two brothers; he wasn't letting his parents architect his life. Then I picked up from where I left in Cancun reliving some of the sordid details about my nuclear family.

"Sorry to hear about the loss of your father. I'm certain that he would have been proud of you for the woman you have become," he smiled.

"I guess. I don't know if it even matters," I said nonchalantly.

"You seem like you don't have closure with his death," he began to pry.

"I'm good. You never lost a parent so you really can't relate," I said, cutting to the chase.

"You're right, but I did lose my twin brother," he said, shocking me.

"You didn't mention you had a twin. What happened?" I asked once again without thinking.

"Another day," he smiled.

"Oh, ok," I replied bewildered and a little wounded. I shared with him. Was he too good to share with me?

"I thought we were sharing," I rebuffed. "The Black girl can share her life with Dr. Phil, but he can't share with her. Such a double standard. White people," I hissed.

"My lack of pigmentation has nothing to do with my right to share my life and its details with whom I choose. You have a race chip on your shoulder and waiting for the slightest wind to touch it. Unfortunately for you, I don't have much time to give to people who don't want to be judged, but are always judging others," he stated firmly taking out his wallet to pay for the meal.

"You don't have to do that," I grabbed his hand. "I invited you to dinner. I'm sorry I offended you."

"You insulted me. You don't know Larry, all you see is this white guy. Isn't it?" he asked, looking sincere and transparent.

"Yes," I took a deep breath. Was I a bitch?

"I see a beautiful woman who I wanted to get to know better, but probably won't be able to because she can't see me," he said, getting ready to stand up.

"Larry, please don't go. I am sorry. I shouldn't have said what I did. I was upset about you inquiring about my closure concerning my dad's death and then not sharing about your brother," I said with no filter.

"Thank you for being transparent. I accept your apology," he sat back down.

I was happy. This man was getting ready to walk out on me. Did I just beg him to stay?

"I normally don't beg a man to stay with me," I said, feeling the need to justify my actions.

"I thought you were being a decent human being apologizing for insulting me. I didn't know you were begging me to stay. Fatima, please don't let your ego and our races get in the way our burgeoning friendship," he said, reaching across the table for my hand.

"Dually noted. Larry, I see the world through the lenses of who I am, a Black woman. That will never change," I said unapologetically.

"I am not asking you to change who you are, but see beyond who you are. Only in America are you a Black woman. Everywhere else, you are an American woman. Race was invented for socioeconomic reasons to exploit resources and justify racism. Where else in the world are people known by color? What is a white person or a Black person? There are not black, red, white, or yellow spirits. There is one spirit that dwells on the inside of us, and that is God's spirit if we allow Him.

"Was it God's spirit that let white men enslave, kill, and exploit my ancestors?" I asked, wondering what he would say to defend his people.

"We all are born sinners and sinners do things after the lusts of their flesh. Also, as sure as there is a God, there is also an enemy. He steals, kills, and destroys. He has no color or nationality," he said unmoved.

"Well, there seems to be a lot of blue-eyed devils," I laughed.

"In most major cities, including this one and yours, brown eyes are killing brown eyes," he said still unmoved.

"But there is a reason why," I said, getting ready to explain.

"There is a reason why there is a disproportionate amount of Black men in both prisons and in the homes of the women who bear their children. There are reasons why poor, white men hate Black men, but lust after Black women. There are reasons why the Black vote is contained in the Democratic Party; why Democrats run most major cities and have failing public school systems."

"What are you trying to say? I'm a Democrat, and I suppose you are a Republican after all of that," I pouted.

"I'm neither. No party gets my vote, and every candidate must earn my vote," he said, putting me to silence.

"Most Europeans bought West Africans and made them into slaves although some raided and stole. Africans sold Africans that were their prisoners and captives from battles into slavery for their benefit. Most Atlantic slave traders were Portuguese, British, French, Spanish, and Dutch and in that order. So when you say whites be specific. There are more nationalities that share my skin tone than those I stated. So, it's not all white people. Furthermore, the majority of slaves that were sold went to South America, not North America. Any way you can look at it this way, the wages of sin is death. Africans died coming across the Atlantic, but Africans are still dying today because of the sins of their forefathers," he said.

"But your people exploited not only us but also the American Indians," I said, becoming infuriated by his history lesson. "They used religion and God to lure Indians into genocide."

"My people? Once again, some of that narrative is true. But a half truth is a whole lie. No different than the narratives that so called "Black leaders" tell today to keep Blacks sleep. These "leaders" are making deals that they benefit from at the expense of their people. These Black leaders have stacked the cards against poor, uneducated Blacks as a form of elitism so they can show their superiority," he said so assured.

"And how do you know that Professor White?"

"It's all around you. Look at Baltimore. A Black mayor shut down libraries in the "City That Reads." A Black superintendent of schools hired a bunch of her unqualified sorority sisters to teach inner city youth," he spewed.

"What are you talking about? That sounds crazy," I insisted with disbelief.

"I just sent you a link to a book if you cared to be informed," he said, making me feel ignorant of my own race.

"Everything you said still does not negate American History and the wrong that was done," I simply stated with a smirk.

"Facts are what happened, but what is the truth. Would you prefer to be Black living in the United States of America, as ugly as it was or sometimes still can be? Or would you rather live in West Africa, with its history and present as ugly as it was or still can be?

"Shit, I don't want any part of Africa, now or ever!" I said with all seriousness.

"Well, I'm glad you're here. Please don't take this philosophical jousting as any slight against your race. I am humbled and in awe of the resilience of Blacks in America. I know there are people who hate you for no other reason other than that you are Black. I know there are some who disrespect you because you are a woman. I know there are some who are intimidated by your candor, sass, and intelligence."

"Are you still talking about Blacks," I asked as he seemed to have switched the topic to me.

"You, indeed. I am talking to you. I'm glad I stayed, and we had this convo. I'm glad you let Larry in for a second despite his melanin deficiency," he said as we both laughed.

"You're alright with me Larry. This wasn't as bad as I thought it was going to be given our previous conversation," I sighed.

"I have tough skin," he started, but I remembered something he said.

"You're not a poor white man who hates black men, so why do you like black women?"

"I like women in general," he smiled. "I was smitten by you because of your looks. Your smile and the sparkle in your eyes. Your facial expressions."

"My facial expressions?" I inquired.

"Yes, like the one you just made. Your face betrays you; it tells how you feel whether you choose to share how you feel or not. I love that. It shows a genuine and transparent person," he smiled.

"So, how do I feel now?" I asked, feeling intrigued by his analysis.

"I have piqued your curiosity by my statements. Right or wrong?"

"Maybe," I smiled.

"You're not good at lying or hiding your feelings either," he said, looking right through me.

"Yes, I'm working on that," I agreed.

"Don't work too hard. I like that about you. I saw it on the first day," he winked.

"Even when I'm talking about race?" I asked hesitantly.

"As long as you're honest and remember I am Larry, not the entire white race as if there was some "white race," he said with a serious tone.

"Duly noted! I just ask you to be remindful that I am Black, and we still live in a nation where I am judged by the color of my skin and not the content of my character," I sighed.

"Touché, so do I," he sighed as he looked deeply into my eyes.

A weird feeling flowed through my body as we stared at each other in silence. Uncomfortable yet at peace, I felt like I had a glimpse into Larry's soul. I felt like it said to me, *"please don't judge me because of the color of my skin."* I was scared and soothed all in one gasping breath.

"Nakedness has no color: this can come as news only to those who have never covered, or been covered by, another naked human being," he said as he kept his eyes in direct connection with mine. "James Baldwin."

"Is there something you want to tell me, Larry," I blurted with no refrain.

"Yes, two things! I like you a lot and good night," he said, knocking the air out of me.

"What the h…," I began to utter before he grabbed my hand and kissed it.

"I've gotta go. Thank you for the pleasure of your company. I hope I can see you again soon. Being around you makes me feel alive," he winked.

"Are you serious?" I asked still utterly flabbergasted by his statement about liking me.

"Yes, I must go," he laughed.

"Who does that? Tell a girl he likes her and then leaves her with no conversation?" I asked impatiently.

"There's nothing I think I should add to what I stated," he said as he stood to leave.

"Goodnight Fatima," he said, leaving me with my mouth slightly ajar.

Did I just get played? What type of Mack-game did this white boy have? What was I supposed to say? Why would this country club southern boy like an urban bougie ghetto girl? Why am I even questioning why he likes me? This is ridiculous! I am Fatima Antoinette Crosby! Why wouldn't a man like me? Well, a black man? This was too much. I needed to talk to someone with good advice and wisdom. When I got back to my hotel room, I called my grandmother.

"Hey Mama, am I waking you?" I asked, hoping she wasn't sleeping.

"It's never too late. I love hearing your voice," she said, making my heart warm. "What's going on? Who is he?"

"Huh? Why would you ask that? I was calling…," I began to fabricate when she cut to the chase.

"Something or someone is bothering you, and you needed some clarity," she said with no hesitance.

"His name is Larry; he's white; and he says he likes me," I spewed like a water faucet.

"Does Larry know the Lord?" she asked as if none of what I said mattered.

"Yes, he's a Christian and is celibate," I responded not sure of what to say next.

"Why does he like you?" she asked, leaving me bewildered.

"Umm, I don't know," I replied like a child.

"Do you like him?" she asked.

"I think so…I mean I don't know," I replied confused as ever.

"Of course, you like him and what you really want is for someone to tell you it is ok. Baby, it's okay to like Larry. He is a child of God before he is a white man. Just like you are a child of God before you are a Black woman," she said as a matter of fact.

"But, it feels weird," I said still unsure.

"It feels weird to have someone different than you in all regards and aspects like you. Like Fatima for who she is beyond what the eye can see. Baby, let him show why he likes you," she said, putting a calmness in my fluttering heart.

"Does it matter that..." I began.

"Does it matter that he is different? Does it matter he is white? What matters is what we make matter. Sometimes money or the lack thereof matters. Sometimes fidelity or the lack thereof matters. Sometimes time and distance matter. What matters to you should be this moment. This moment when my 25-year-old granddaughter awakens her grandmother at midnight about a guy she "thinks" she likes," she said not mincing her words.

"If he didn't matter, you wouldn't have called me. I don't know the name of any guy you have dated since your senior prom. Give Larry a chance," she said, releasing my inhibitions.

"Thank you, Mama! He's funny and makes me laugh. He also has a deep southern drawl, and it's so cute. He says I'm pretty and asked me not to judge him by the color of his skin, but the content of his character," I said, recounting our encounter.

"Enough said. Next time you call, I want an update about you and Larry," she said before ending the call.

"Yes, Ma'am," I said, ending our call.

Empowered by our conversation, I decided to text him. I really wanted to call him, but I didn't want to bother him. For all I knew, he could have been on a date with another chick.

Me: Hi Larry, what r u doing?

Larry: Working. What are you doing?

Me: Nothing.

Me: Well, I just got off the phone with Mama.

Larry: How is she doing?

Me: Good.

Larry: Well, that's good. How are you?

Me: Good.

Larry: What's up?

Me: Huh?

Larry: One-word answers. What's on your mind?

Me: Nothing.

Before I knew it, the phone rang. It was him. I froze up like a little girl. I wasn't good at playing games and beating around the bush, and he was sensing that I was trying to.

"Hey pretty lady," he said, making my insides gush.

"Hey, you. How are you?" I asked again.

"Ok, let's cut to the chase. What's up. Why are you so cryptic?" he replied.

"Thinking about you, but not trying to bother you. You could have been on a date or something," I said, getting it out.

"But I told you I'm not dating anyone. Do you remember that?" he asked.

"Well, yeah, but," I began.

"There is no, but. I have no reason to lie. I know you have been disappointed and let down by men whose character flaws led them to live debauched lives. However, they both showed you who they were from the beginning; you just chose not to believe them."

"Well, goddamn Larry! Can you be a little gentile as you replay the sordid details of my derailed love life," I insisted.

"You just hurt my feelings. I was texting your ass because I missed you and had just finished talking to Mama about you," I exclaimed while regretting my transparency afterward.

"Well, I miss you too, but please don't accuse me of lying. I'm not perfect, but a liar I am not," he said.

"You miss me?" I replied forgetting everything else he said.

"Yes, I miss you, crazy woman," he laughed.

"Crazy woman? Boy, you ain't seen crazy," I said, recounting some of my crazy moments.

"The devil is a lie," he responded cracking me up.

"What you know about that?" I asked still shocked by his response.

"Girl, I'm from Louisiana. I should be asking you what you know about that," he said, setting the record straight.

"You all alright with me Mr. Martin," I said glad the ice was broken.

"Now back to us missing each other. I would like for you to go somewhere with me on Wednesday night," he said.

"Where and why so cryptic, pray tell," I said, using his words against him.

"Trust me," he demanded.

"What should I wear?" I tried to gather a clue.

"Makes no difference," he answered.

"Ok, I'm going to come in my birthday suit," I jested.

"Come on now. A brother is trying to stay saved," he laughed.

"Bet. I definitely don't want God to strike me down for getting you off the golden path of enlightenment," I joked but serious at the same time.

"He loves you and has plans to prosper you and not harm you. He has plans to give you hope and a future," he said.

"Wow, that was so nice. Where do you come up with these things?" I asked, feeling encouraged by his words.

"Do you have a Bible app on your cell? If not, download one and look up Jeremiah 29:11," he said.

"Well, I don't but I will," I responded while going into my app store. "And yes, to answer your question. I'm down for Wednesday night. I would love to go with you."

"Awesome!" he said, ending our phone call.

When the Bible loaded onto my phone, I searched for Jeremiah 29:11. It read,

"For I know the plans I have for you," declares the Lord, "plans to prosper you and not to harm you, plans to give you hope and a future."

11 | At the Well

On Wednesday night, he picked me up. Clueless, I put on "date wear" not "church wear." Thank God, everyone was casually dressed. The biggest surprise was his church was predominately Black. I could have fainted. I saw a couple of other sprinkles, but they were few and far between. Then, Larry sat near the pulpit. I felt so awkward.

I did not consider myself a religious person. Mama was always praying for us, so I figured her prayers were good enough. Larry told me every person must work out their own salvation. Didn't quite know what he meant, but, in time, I would learn.

That night, the pastor's wife led the service, which was more like a Bible study. She seemed like a happy person, borderline sickening. Two things I was certain of, she loved God, and she believed He loved every one of us. Her sermon came from the book of John. Some woman, who sounded like a hoe, met Jesus at a well. I didn't know where she was going with the story until she started talking about brokenness in families and relationships.

"This woman had these relationships, and the remnants of them were attached to her. If you were raised by a broken parent or parents, you have some shards of the brokenness in you. If you have been in a relationship with a broken person, you have shards of that brokenness. Broken people cut you, sometimes unbeknownst to you. But, there is a blessing in brokenness. It allows Jesus a way to make you whole. Jesus wants you to be whole, and that wholeness can only come through Him."

As she spoke, I began to think about my life, from my parents to all my failed relationships. I felt like there was a spotlight on me, and everyone knew my business. I was very uncomfortable. Was I broken? Amid my internal turmoil, I tuned into her once again when she asked for everyone who knew they were broken and wanted to be made whole to come to the front of the church.

With everyone's eyes closed and heads bowed, I felt like someone was prodding me to go. I didn't want to move because I didn't want anyone to know I was broken. About six people went to the front, and right before she began to pray, she walked off the altar and came over to where Larry and I were sitting.

"It doesn't matter what anyone thinks of you. If your soul is broken, no amount of money or success can mask brokenness. Jesus loves you and died for you. He said what good is it for you to gain the whole world and lose your soul. If you deny Him in front of men, He will deny you in front of the Father."

Tears began to trail my face. I stood up and began to walk, and she grabbed me. I felt my knees weaken. She asked me to raise my hands and began speaking words to me but took the microphone away from her mouth.

"Your road has not been an easy one. Made some bad decisions, but He loves you. He loves you more than anyone you have known and will ever know. You think you are the unlikely candidate for happiness. You are wrong. God wants you to know that love is yours. He is developing an awesome testimony out of your life. God is going to show you the true meaning of love like you have never experienced before. He wants you naked before Him, and He will clothe you with everything you need to become the woman He created you to be. It's ok to have questions, but don't doubt Him or what He is doing in your life."

While I wept and began to lower my hands, she placed her hands on my stomach and started speaking in tongues. Then, she began to utter words I could understand again.

"Satan, you are a liar, and I rebuke you in the name of Jesus. Death, you have no victory, and you have no sting. Nothing will prevail against the blood of Jesus. Jehovah Rapha is healing you right now. She will have double for her trouble in Jesus' name!"

Surreal is the only word that comes to mind when trying to describe how I felt. A warm sensation flowed through my body as I trembled and wept. Next thing I knew, I was waking up on the floor. I didn't remember falling. I had no pain or aches. I could barely look at Larry let alone speak. I felt indescribably different from the inside out. When we arrived at my hotel, Larry opened my door, and as I stood I hugged him tightly around the neck, he hugged me back. It's like he knew what I was going through. A couple of tears rolled down my face, as I tried to refrain.

"It's okay. Let it out. God loves you so much. He has favored you," he said, hugging me tighter.

I cried like a baby. I began to think of all the wrong I had done and now realized He was watching but loved me anyway.

"Larry, I've done some pretty awful things," I cried.

"It's ok. There is no big or small sin with God. He knew what we would do, and He died for us anyway," he said, drying my tears.

He walked me to my room, and we sat down and talked. My head flooded with so many questions. I felt like I had taken the red pill; I was in the Matrix, and my life would never be the same.

"When God calls us out of darkness into the light, life seems unearthly. You are awakened and no longer existing, but living. Christ says He comes that we can have life and have it more abundantly."

"This must be crazy for you. You take a girl to church and then she's weeping like a baby," I said, still in disbelief that I cried in front of Larry and his church.

"No, not at all. It happened to me," he said, smiling.

"What do you mean?" I asked, surprised by his response.

"Damali took me to church, and I gave my life to Christ that Sunday, New Year's Day," he replied.

I was shocked. Damali was his ex-girlfriend that he spoke of highly.

"Wow, are you serious? Is that why you two broke up?" I had to know.

"Once you are connected to God's Spirit, He will guide you in all areas, even your relationships. We both came to terms that we were not the ones for each other. Letting her go was hard, but it was right. Now we're both free to be with who God has chosen for us," he said.

"No big argument or drama?" I asked in disbelief.

"We were friends, so there was no drama," he replied.

"If you had something so good, why end it? Shouldn't you marry a friend?" I asked even more interested in his logic.

"You marry who God has placed in your life, not who you place. I wanted Damali, but she's not who God had for me," he said assuredly.

"How will you know? Will God speak to you in an audible voice? There she is, she's the one," I said in a James Earl Jones voice.

"How did you know to surrender tonight? Even against everything that was dissuading you to go the altar, why did you go?" he asked.

"I couldn't help it. There was this undeniable feeling. I felt like my life depended on it. It was something I have never experienced," I said.

"Bingo! So, you already know," he smiled.

"Well, you shouldn't be wasting your time with me," I shook my head. "You need a woman who is on that level. I'm more like that hoe at the damn well except I'm at the swimming pool. She had five men compared to my 50. I have had five abortions and I…"

"Shhh…Stop! You are fearfully, wonderfully, and custom-made by God. The woman at the well didn't know her value until Christ came into her life. Stop undervaluing yourself because of past decisions," he said sternly.

He didn't flinch when I mentioned all the awful things I had done.

"Thank you, Larry," I said as tears filled my eyes.

"Your latter days will be better than your former days. Believe that, Fatima," he said as he kissed my hand and departed.

From that day forward, I began my journey, my *Bildungsroman*. My goal was to become the woman that God created me to be. God had a funny sense of humor on how He orchestrated things, but I was not going to be a fool and let this opportunity pass me.

I became used to my dual life, one in DC and the other in Atlanta, although I missed Larry when I traveled back north. Work was good, but I didn't care for my director, Ellen. She was a control freak and borderline racist. She made a point of calling me sister-girl when she gave me feedback. A couple of times, she asked me if I wore a weave and could she feel my hair. I was glad to escape her when I went to Atlanta. However, one week, she flew down with me and wanted us to have dinner, but Larry and I already had plans. He said he would join us. I told her my friend was dining with us and she assumed it was a girl.

"Hey Fatima," she said, standing to hug me. "Where is your friend?"

"Parking," I replied.

"I took the liberty of ordering some sushi rolls for us and some Sake. I hope you don't mind. Do you eat sushi? I really don't know of any Soul Food restaurants here in the ATL," she said, smiling as if that shit was funny.

"Well, actually I love Maki, some Nigiri, but I'm not a fan of Sashimi. As far as Soul Food, I'm particular," I responded, trying not to lose my cool. However, Ellen was distracted.

"OMG. I would love to have his babies, and he is coming our way!" she exclaimed.

"Hello ladies," Larry said.

"Hello to you. Do you want to join us? You don't mind, Fatima, do you?" she asked while ogling him.

"Ellen, please meet my friend, Larry," I said.

"Excuse me. You're Fatima's friend?" she inquired, looking completely shocked.

"That is I. Larry Martin," he said, extending his hand.

"No offense, but are you gay?" she asked out of left field.

"Um, no. Why'd you ask?" he responded for us both.

"Well, this is Atlanta, and you are friends with Fatima," she said, making my blood boil.

"Are you serious right now? The only way an attractive man can be with a black woman is for him to be gay? Is that what you're alluding to, Ellen?" I demanded.

"Well, let's not get our panties all up in a bunch," she insisted. "Just a harmless mistake."

"It's always harmless when whites do it, but let that bullshit come from a black person, and y'all would have a heart attack," I vented.

"Fatima, I am sorry if I offended you. It's really no big deal," she said, looking at Larry as if she needed support.

"Ignorance covers the walls of this nation, and a teachable moment like this will help tear it down," he said, calming the moment as the food arrived at our table.

"As I told Fatima, I took the liberty of ordering food and drinks," she said, cheesing in his face.

"I'm not a fan of sake or sushi in general. I had planned to take Fatima to a Soul Food restaurant," he added as he examined the food.

"Well, she's very particular about her Soul Food," she said in a sarcastic tone.

Before I could get the words out, Larry enlightened her.

"So am I. I'm from Louisiana, and I'm the one who feigns for Soul Food. Fatima is more adventuresome than I. Give me some greens, yams, black-eyed peas with some ham hocks, and then we're talking."

"Yuck! You are too lean to eat that kind of stuff," she said.

"I don't eat it every day, but I do indulge," he replied.

"So, what do you do, Larry?" she inquired.

"I'm an attorney," he replied.

"Where? For who?" she continued.

"For a Fortune 100, but we didn't come here to discuss me," he said, answering and closing her interrogation.

We were able to have some decent conversations given that I spoke more to Larry than to Ellen. She became Larry's groupie and cosigned to everything he said. The thirst was real. It seemed at any moment, she could have jumped onto his lap. I endured as much as I could before Larry seemingly read my mind and ended the evening. Ellen attempted to hug Larry, but he firmly extended his hand to her. That one move made up for the entire night.

"You weren't lying. You have your hands full with her," he jested.

"You thought I was lying?" I asked, bothered by his statement.

"Figure of speech. I'm not the enemy here," he said.

"I'm sorry. This is the bullsh...the bull I have to go through," I said, trying not to cuss. "You don't have to deal with racism."

"Not directly, but indirectly. It's real, from schools to boardrooms. That's why I volunteer at organizations, so I can equip young black men who do not have access to the same things their counterparts do."

"Do you want to have children?" I asked, not wanting to assume anything.

"Absolutely! I love children!" he exclaimed. "And you?"

"Ditto, I would love to have my own," I said, being as transparent as possible.

"What do you think about adoption?" he asked completely out of left field.

"I don't. Do you?" I probed.

"Yes, I am open to it," he said, smiling.

"Larry, please don't take this the wrong way, but you are nice as hell. Much nicer and more generous than I."

"According to who? How you view yourself up to this moment or when you look at Fatima's limitless possibilities?" he asked, beaming.

"I guess at this moment. Just being around you has me wide open. I am saying and thinking things I didn't know I was capable of comprehending. It's like that phrase, being born again, is real. I truly feel a renewed sense of self. I just don't want to disappoint you or me for that matter."

"You won't. One of the things I love about you is your authenticity. It makes me feel at home. I know I could trust you with my life," he said, blowing my mind.

"Love? One of the things you love about me?" I asked, already knowing the answer.

"Yes, I love you, and I would like the honor of courting you to discover if we are compatible for marriage," he said with such tenderness and humility in his voice.

"You are blowing my mind right now," I said before he interrupted me.

"It's ok; I'm a big boy. I would still like to be friends," he said, bowing out gracefully.

"Um, hell no! I love you too, Boo, and yes, absolutely! Consider us courting," I said, grabbing his hand.

An overpowering magnetism drew us together in each other's arms as we kissed for the first time. It felt like nothing I had ever experienced. Love felt like a stranger and family all at the same time. Larry's arms felt like forever, and that's where I wanted to be. I had a man that loved me, not just for what I could do for him or how many times he could climax in my coochie, or to simply make him look good. Larry had it going on and didn't need me, but he wanted me, and that was a good feeling. He had a heart of gold, will power made of platinum, and the character of a flawless diamond. I don't know why God favored me, despite all my sins, and sent me Larry, but I wasn't going to mess it up with second-guessing. I read in one of my daily devotions that when you become a new creation through

Jesus, old things are expired, and we are to embrace the new in faith, believing that God has ordered our footsteps.

12 | I Do

The week after Larry and I committed, my mother wanted to visit me the next time I was home. She met with Mr. Peter and needed my advice. Although I didn't feel qualified to give her advice, Larry suggested that many times people just need someone to listen. When she came in, she remarked on the last time she visited me, which was shortly after I moved. I took her on a tour, and she was full of compliments, from the decorum to my furniture selections.

"I am very proud of you, Fatima. You have exquisite taste," she said, nodding her head with approval.

"Why thank you, Mother, I mean Mom," I said, hoping I didn't offend.

"It's ok. You have called me Mother all of your life. Mother or Mom, I know you love me," she said, hugging me.

"This is still new for me. All of this, even you hugging me like you do and ending every call with I love you," I said, reminiscing about the last couple of months since she and I had our *Come-To-Meet-Jesus* conversation.

"Life is too short. Words left unsaid and hugs not given are often interpreted as apathy. Before I leave this Earth, I have to let those who matter most, matter most. Does that make sense?" she asked.

"Understood. So, what happened at lunch with Mr. Peter?" I asked, cutting to the chase.

"We met at a restaurant, but neither of us was hungry. We spoke about how Andrew and he were adjusting. I never considered the stigma associated with someone dying from drug overdoses or suicide. He said Andrew wasn't quite a well-adjusted young man because Priscilla used him as an emotional tampon. When Peter tried to intervene, Andrew turned on him, blaming him for her condition. Our affair appeared to overshadow Priscilla's affair with your dad. It made me feel guilty," she said.

"Mom, Priscilla was a basket case before you and after you. What happened to her is not your fault. Did you tell him that Maurice is his son?" I said, trying to get to the meat.

"No, that's what I need to discuss with you. Peter told me he never stopped loving me," she said with tears in her eyes.

"Wow! You should be happy. Why are you sad?" I asked completely oblivious.

"He loves me based on a memory, a memory of a young lady he could trust. When he finds out the truth, I fear all of that love will vanish as the words depart from my lips," she said, weeping.

"Mom, you two were together in college, and he chose a career that took him away from you. Settling for less than you both deserved, you married shards of glass, a hoe in your case and a psycho for Mr. Peter.

You were broken by your unions, which lead to committing adultery with each other. When the affair ended, you two were subsequently punished by your broken spouses cheating on you with each other. The whole thing is just fuc..I mean messed up," I said.

"So, here I am today in front of you still broken, bleeding, and longing for true love," she said, weeping harder.

"That brokenness, Mom, wasn't meant for a man to fill. There's only one who can make us whole," I responded.

"Please let me know because I will pay whatever it costs to meet him or her," she said with such desperation in her voice.

"Jesus Christ," I said, watching her gasp for air.

"Are you serious right now?" she asked, suspended in disbelief.

"Absolutely, unequivocally serious!" I exclaimed.

"Please explain this because I am at a loss," she said, looking at me with an agog stare.

"Please don't take what I am about to say as a slight against you, but broken parents raise broken children. I am the byproduct of Dad's and your brokenness. I never knew how much until I started cutting myself," I said.

"Oh no, honey! You've been cutting yourself?" she exclaimed with horror.

"Hell no! Not cutting myself in that sense but the abortions, promiscuity, and irreverent attitude. When I was able to take a look in the mirror and see who I became, she differed greatly from the image of who I thought I would be," I said.

"How did you come to the realization?" she inquired.

"Larry," I simply stated.

"The white guy? So, it's getting serious between you two?" she asked.

"He's White, like I am Black, however, yes Larry," I responded, realizing that I didn't use that adjective anymore when describing him.

"How did he do that?" she became intrigued.

"He's not broken, and he sets the boundaries by which he will not let a broken person cut him. At one point I didn't realize the shape I was in, but the closer I came to Christ the more I began to see my cracks," I said, remembering some of the painful purging moments Larry and I shared.

"You talk about Jesus as if He is alive and not a historical figure," she responded.

"Mom, do you believe in the Bible?" I asked.

"I guess, but I haven't really read it. When I left my parents' home, I decided not to be as religious as them. So, I see church as something you do on special occasions," she said sincerely.

"Jesus is the third person of the God-head, the trinity. The Bible tells us He died and rose again on the third day for the remission or forgiveness of our sins. Whosoever shall call on the name of the Lord shall be saved. Mom, a man cannot save you from Hell. Relying on an imperfect man to love you will result in an imperfect love. We as women create our own hell by living with unrealistic expectations. A man without Christ will never heal what only God can," I said, feeling emboldened by His spirit.

"Please help me. What do I have to do to be saved?" she cried.

I took her by the hands and prayed a simple prayer with her, asking Jesus to come into her life as her Lord and Savior. We both cried and embraced each other. As we composed ourselves, I wanted to get back to the source for which she needed advice.

"Mom, you said you needed my advice. Why?" I asked, once again being direct.

"Whether I should tell Peter about Maurice," she said, looking scared.

"Absolutely. I know you fear rejection because you have suffered a lot of it. However, God hasn't given us a spirit of fear, but of love, power, and a sound mind. Truth makes people free. You can't abide by lies; they will kill you. Look at Priscilla," I said with no chaser.

"Wow! I am absolutely amazed, Fatima. You are phenomenal. Your words feel like water to my parched soul," she said, making me smile.

"Did I say something funny?" she inquired.

"I am just quoting the Bible. The Word of God says that when we believe in Jesus, rivers of living water flow from our hearts," I answered. I was surprised at how much I had learned in such a short time. At the end of my mother's visit, she said she was going to tell Mr. Peter the truth. At that moment, for the first time in my life, I was proud of my mother. I ended the evening sharing with Larry what transpired, and he told me he was proud of me. I felt like it was the absolute best day of my life until time would prove me wrong.

The next couple of months seemed to move really fast. Intentionally, I disconnected from most people in my life, except my mother and grandmother. It was like I went into a cocoon to develop and solidify this new direction I had chosen for my life. When I did speak to my close friends, I kept it brief. I didn't want any naysayers or skeptics ruining what Larry called my "magnum opus."

Larry and I saw each other often when I was in Atlanta, and he came to DC a couple of times for work. I decided to join his church and began taking "Life Enrichment" classes. They were for people who were new to Christian living. I learned a lot quickly and was amazed how ignorant I was to the spiritual side of life. I was a babe, but I was enjoying being fed.

"Hey, Gee. Girl, I'm so happy to see you," I said, entering Gee's apartment. We hadn't seen each other in a while.

"Yeah, it's the end of September. Although we have spoken, I haven't seen you since the beginning of August," she said, pointing out my unexcused leave of absence.

"I know. I'm sorry. Larry and I are always doing something. Some weeks, he's up here for work, and I'm down there a lot. But, you know how that goes," I said, remembering when she was dating John, who she still hadn't spoken to since their breakup.

"No not really," she sighed as if she was bothered. "I'm glad things are working out."

"We'll see," I smiled. "So, Vince didn't work out either, huh?"

"No, but something good came out of it."

"Oh really, like what?" I inquired.

"I've been going to church for about a month now."

"That's great, girl. Vince's church?"

"No, I've been going to a different one every Sunday. I'm searching for the right place."

"Well, I have a little secret to let you in on," I said about to burst.

"What? You're not..."

"Oh, hell no! I've been going to church since we got back from our vacation in July."

"Stop playing! Are you serious?" she looked astonished and in total disbelief.

"I know...I'm a little shocked myself. But, yeah. Our first date, so to speak, was a midweek service at Larry's church. Here's the shocker, it's predominately Black. I think Larry is blacker than I am, girl," I laughed.

"Well, good for you and kudos for Larry. Sometimes, life is better experienced when you're out of your comfort zone," she said, reassuring me.

"You can say that again. Larry is so not me. He's white, southern, polite, and conservative, but, Giselle, he makes me so happy. His calm approach to things is so refreshing. I have never in my life had chemistry with a man that, number one, wasn't Black and, number two, crazy like me."

"Probably because you never opened yourself up to the idea," she said.

"Can I tell you another secret?" I was on a roll.

"Go ahead. You seem to be on a roll!" she laughed.

"We're celibate. Well actually, he's been celibate since he gave his life to the Lord about two years ago."

"Are you serious?" she asked with disbelief.

"Look at my face," I said with complete seriousness.

"You are serious. Boy, I don't know what to say."

"Me either. Now, it is extremely hard at times, but he tries to limit compromising situations. So, he doesn't stay over and leaves at a decent time. We spend more time outside of our homes than in them. That's why I'm always on the go, and I am really enjoying myself," I smiled proudly.

"That is really great," she said, nodding her head approvingly once again.

"I never told you this, but when you were dating John, I was green with envy, girl, about the way he treated you. How he held out for you. The little and the big things he did to show you that you were special," I shared, being totally transparent.

"Really! You were jealous?"

"Who wouldn't be? I never thought that shh...I mean crap would happen to me. I'm trying not to curse. But anyway, I feel like now it's my turn. Someone actually thinks I'm special enough to treat me like it. I can't believe I of all people can actually experience some degree of happiness, and with a white man."

"Are you bothered by him being white? I hear you keep mentioning it," she interrogated.

"We do get some stares, but I guess the biggest issue is me. I feel sort of like a hypocrite. You know all the god-awful things I have said about white people, and now I'm dating one. It just seems like a cruel contradiction of sorts," I rebutted once again in transparency.

"My mother has always taught us to rid our vocabularies of the words always and never, because when it's all said and done, God will have the final say," she said.

"After allowing myself to be treated like nothing, it feels good to finally be with someone who treats me like something. It's like I don't deserve it."

"Do you believe in coincidence or destiny? Meeting Larry is no coincidence but a part of a bigger plan," she said, trying to give me a greater perspective.

"Sometimes, I feel like he's Jesus and I'm Mary Magdalene," I blurted.

"What Mary was prior to her meeting Christ wasn't relevant. Our Pastor just taught this past Sunday that Christ didn't come for the healthy but for the sick. Fatima, I think you have to forgive yourself. Larry could be the best thing since sliced bread, but if you don't cast the demons of your past out of your life and heart, you will sabotage any future you two may have. I'm happy about your relationship with Larry and your going to church. You know I only want the best for you," she said, hugging me.

"For the first time in my life, I do too. But enough about me, how are you? I'm sorry none of your dates panned out," I said, purposely changing the topic before I started crying.

"They just weren't meant to be. I'm fortunate to have had these dating misfortunes if that makes sense."

"Boy, do I know! So basically, none of them could compare to my boy," I said, inferring John.

"Your boy?"

"John...John. You do remember him, don't you?"

"I'll probably never forget him, but life does go on."

"You never did tell me what happened," I inquired.

"Do you have some time?"

"Sure..."

"Well, it all started when I went to visit him before Christmas..."

Giselle and I talked into the wee hours of the morning. She told me about finding out that he had a child, and that she thought he has AIDS. When she found out and broke up with him, she realized she was pregnant and aborted the baby. We cried together, laughed, and eventually fell asleep in her living room.

Shortly after Thanksgiving, Giselle ran into John's sister, Lori, who told her the child was not John's biological daughter but his deceased brother's. His brother had AIDS and committed suicide, and John was the only person who knew he had a daughter. She was HIV positive, and her mother didn't have much money, so John adopted her. You can't make this shit up. I was in awe. I knew he was a noble dude, but my God! Confused on what she should do, Giselle took my advice and reached out to John to try to make amends. Her first attempt failed, but then she was invited to his sister's wedding in Rhode Island. The only way she would attend was if I went with her. She was so full of pride; I didn't want her to block her blessing in disguise.

It is utterly amazing what friends do for each other. There is no way in heaven or hell I would ever fly to Rhode Island for anything not business-related, but I did in the name of love. The whole time I was there, I missed Larry. This would be our first Christmas and I couldn't wait to get back to DC to see him. He was forgoing seeing his family and spending Christmas with mine. He met my mother and Maurice on a couple of occasions when he was in the area. However, on Christmas day, he would meet Mama. They had seen each other via iPhone, but now they were going to meet face-to-face.

"Babe, are you on the way?" I asked, anxiously awaiting his arrival to my mother's.

"I'm here," he said, coming up behind me and hugging me. I screamed, jumped, and hugged him all at once.

"I missed you so much! Merry Christmas, baby," I said, melting like chocolate.

"I missed you more," he said, kissing my forehead and giving me a small, but exquisitely wrapped gift.

"Oh wait," I said, running to the tree to get his gifts.

"Open mine first. Tell the truth; you won't hurt my feelings if you don't like them," I said, hoping he would.

He opened the first gift, which was a sleek leather iPhone case with his monogram. The second was the newest iPhone. By his reaction, I did well. I was happy; I had sealed the *Girlfriend of the Year* award.

"Now, it's my turn," he said, placing a small box in my hand. It was a silver charm bracelet with three charms.

"This is nice," I said, looking at the cross, angel, and circle.

"The cross is so you will always remember Christ in Christmas. The angel is what you are to me. You are a blessing; through our relationship, I want to be the best version of me possible. You make me exhibit all the characteristics Christ says I should have."

"What is the circle with the diamonds?" I asked puzzled.

"A circle means infinite, never-ending. That's my love and commitment to you," he said as tears began to fill my eyes. "Diamonds are strong and have the highest value. That's what you are to me, a diamond," he said as he got on one knee and reached into his pocket.

"What…What?" I began to say and then looked up and saw my family surrounding us. My mother and grandmother were both crying.

"In case you can't see the ring on your charm, I bought you this one," he said, opening a small box. It was a beautiful emerald cut diamond ring.

"God showed His love toward me when He gave me you. Please take this ring as a symbol of my commitment to you, strong and never-ending. Love never fails. Fatima, will you marry me?" he asked.

"Yes! Yes!" I cried as tears filled the room.

He stood and kissed me. I was going to be Larry's wife. Larry loved me and wanted to spend his life with me. Feelings of peace and happiness overtook my mind, body, and soul. I would have failed as a fortune-teller because I would have never predicted this for me. I was looking forward to marrying Larry and having a family together. The thought of being a mother used to scare me, but with Larry, I felt empowered to do whatever my heart desired. I was marrying the man I loved, and before long, we would work on building a family.

13 | The Beat Goes On

A week after Larry proposed to me, John proposed to Giselle. Everything seemed to pan out for both my best friend and me, well at least for a little while. The same night John proposed to Giselle, his parents and daughter were in a fatal car accident. They went from being reunited and happy, to distant and sad. Giselle said she tried being there for John, but some anchor woman he dated while they were apart was taking front and center. Against my counsel, Giselle backed away from John during his time of bereavement. She said she would be there once he came through and acted like he wanted to be with her.

"Giselle, I don't think you need to worry about Kennedy. All of your energy and concern needs to be directed toward John. He's going to be your husband. He will always remember this moment in time. Anyone can be there for a person when they are on top of the world, but they will remember the people who were there when the world was on top of them," I said, trying to give her a better perspective.

"I don't care how much grieving he is doing, he should have checked Kennedy at that damn hospital and let her know I am his woman!" she said, doused in her selfishness.

"Your engagement should speak volumes, friend," I said, shaking my head. I wanted to choke her. She was self-absorbed. I pitied John and hoped he knew what he was getting himself into with my primadonna friend.

"You think I'm a primadonna, don't you?" she asked, reading my mind.

"You said it! If it was Larry, I would be his Charmin and his pillow. If you aren't there for him during this season, I'm afraid of what will happen," I warned her.

"It'll be alright. John isn't going anywhere," she declared with confidence.

Within months, their relationship shredded like Mozzarella. As John's grief increased, so did Giselle's distance. It was the strangest thing I had ever witnessed. I tried to be there for Giselle, but it was hard to see her viewpoint since her loss couldn't compare to John's. I would discuss it periodically with Larry to obtain his thoughts and perspective on it.

"It's always easier from the outside looking in to see others' missteps and poor decisions. The real test is when it happens to us. What would we do? John and Giselle just reunited the night of the tragedy. Tragedies will either bring people together or tear them apart, especially when you are not grounded in God," he said.

"Both of them found Christ and go to church," I replied.

"Finding Christ does not make you immune from being human. If you find Him, that's the first step, but then you have to learn how to walk with and talk to Him. That's a whole other story and level of relationship," he said, making valid points.

"I'm a babe in the Lord, but I don't see letting anything get in the way of me marrying you unless you completely showed me that you are not the person I believed you to be, I said assuredly. Outside of that, nothing and no one will stop me from becoming Mrs. Larry Martin!"

"Sometimes, things happen beyond our control to tip our boats. Some people drown and some swim," he said with compassion, never judging either John or Giselle.

"Well, baby, you have a swimmer," I said as I hugged him.

Since we became engaged, our life was a whirlwind. We set a date, found a venue, and asked our friends to be in our wedding. I would soon be Fatima Martin and no longer Crosby. I was offered a job in Atlanta to be a Vice President of Marketing for a Fortune 100. We started house hunting in Atlanta and considered areas based on schools in preparation for our family. Things were great except for some uncomfortable moments with both family and friends. I met some of Larry's friends and spoke with his parents on the phone. Every time Larry wanted to take me home to meet everyone, something came up with either his parents' or my schedule. However, I finally made it to Louisiana to meet the Martins. I felt like they were coping with the fact that I was Black but still somewhat in shock.

His mother, Lara, was from Texas and met his father, Bob, at Tulane where they both went to undergrad. From their union, they had three sons with Larry being the youngest at 31. All went to top-tiered private schools. Robert, the eldest, was a doctor and Kyle, the middle son, was a lawyer. They both were married and lived in New Orleans.

The Martins lived in Slidell, Louisiana which was located about 45 minutes away from New Orleans, in the southeastern part of St. Tammany Parrish. The day we arrived, the Martins planned a family dinner. Mrs. Martin was indeed the matron of the family, and her sons acquiesced to her suggestions and demands. I was hoping this wasn't going to be a problem between her and me. I wasn't one for taking orders and saying "yes" to just appease someone. When speaking on the phone, she was full of ideas for the wedding and kept saying how we should get married at their home. I didn't accept or reject; I told her my mother had some ideas also, and given that I was from DC, I hadn't considered getting married elsewhere. Larry was nonchalant; he said he was fine with whatever I chose.

When we arrived, both sons and their families were there. Although their house was built in the 70s, it was a pristine 22,000 sq. ft. waterfront Antebellum South house that sat on 10 acres of sprawling lush land. It seemed to have endless rooms, an artesian well, pool, and cabana with a kitchen and bath, carriage house with an apartment, boathouse, and 5-car garage with an apartment. The groundskeeper was pruning flower beds as we parked. Mrs. Martin was standing outside waiting for us.

"Hola, Larry," the man said, waving at Larry. "Ella es muy bonita!"

"Gracias, Hector," Larry waved back to him. "Ella va a ser mi esposa."

"Seems like you already have a fan, Fatima," Mrs. Martin said, greeting us.

"Hello, Mrs. Martin," I said, extending my hand.

"Call me Lara, and we're huggers around here," she said, hugging me.

"How was the drive?" she asked Larry as she hugged him.

"It was nice. Glad we drove instead of flying," he replied as he got the luggage.

"Everyone is here and excited to meet Fatima," she said as we walked inside.

We walked through the house to go to the back where everyone was hanging at the pool. Mr. Martin was the first to greet me. He had a serious, but pleasant disposition. Next, I met Robert, his wife, Lynn, and their two small children. Last, I met Kyle and his wife, Melissa, who were expecting their first child. Melissa complimented me on my shape and talked about how much she couldn't wait to get back into the gym.

Our time with his family was easygoing for the most part. His mother and sisters-in-law drilled me with questions from my life, family, and the wedding. Although they asked what I wanted, they all made references to what they did and what they liked. I said I liked white roses, and Melissa said she liked sunflowers and thought that would be pretty. I said I wanted a small wedding; they spoke of everyone they had to invite. I managed to bridle my tongue as long as I could, but when the conversation changed to Larry and me, I could no longer hold back.

"You know, you two should start working on children right away. Larry has some catching up to do," Lynn said, looking at her children and Melissa's stomach.

"We're going to take our time. Having children isn't something we want to rush into; it's not a competition," I said, smiling.

"It's not, but these Martin boys are extremely competitive. Melissa and I were both homecoming queens and come from pretty good sized families," she said, sounding so superficial.

"I graduated from Ole Miss, and Lynn graduated from Tulane," Melissa added as if she said something noteworthy.

"What is Ole Miss?" I inquired obliviously.

"OMG! It's one of the best schools down here in the South," Melissa laughed sarcastically.

"I'm sorry. What are your schools ranked?" I asked given that I wasn't familiar with either.

"They're pretty up there," Lynn rebutted with sarcasm.

"My bad. I normally rate schools on their ranking nationally, not regionally," I said, trying to refrain.

"I'm not familiar with the University of Virginia," Melissa said.

"Thomas Jefferson built my school. Edgar Allan Poe, don't know if you know of him, but he attended my school. News anchor, Katie Couric, attended my school as well. Oh, and it's ranked in the top 25 universities in the country. Its business school is in the top 15," I smiled, looking at their mouths ajar as I checked them.

"Well, well now we have us a genius here. Just make sure you use all of that when building a family with Larry," Lynn said as she stood to walk away.

"Lynn, before you leave, I want to tell you something so that we are clear on where we stand," I said, trying to temper myself.

"Yes, dear," she said in a patronizing fashion.

"You don't have to like me or approve of me because it makes no difference to me. However, what you're going to do is respect me. Larry didn't bring home a little monkey from the zoo or a girl off a pole. I don't need advice about Larry or our family because that's our business and I don't appreciate people in it unless they're invited," I said.

"Sorry, if you were offended, Fatima. Don't quite know what a monkey or a girl on the pole has to do with anything. You people are so sensitive and walk around with a chip on your shoulders. Yes, you and Larry do have your business, but remember, darling, when you marry, it's not just the individual; it's the family as well. Is there anything else you would like to get off your chest?" Lynn said nonchalantly.

"What did you mean by you people?" I asked, assuming she meant Blacks.

"Northerners! You think you all are so much better than everyone else!" she said.

I was stunned. I thought in race, and she thought in region.

"You look shocked. What did you think I meant," she said, and then Melissa gave her a look.

"OMG! I don't care if you're Black. I have a Black friend and co-workers," she said, giving me the quintessential white response when faced with the topic of race.

"You know what, Lynn, we're good. Just to be clear…"

Bitch is what was on the tip of my tongue, but I nodded no instead. I hated when people tried me and then acted as though they didn't. I wanted to cuss both of them out, but I didn't want to embarrass Larry or myself. I was a new creature in Christ; I wanted to do better. I needed to be better. Our pastor said we have a light that the world needs to see. At times, I felt like mine was a nightlight. When Larry walked in and asked how I was doing, I just lied and said okay. There is a girl-code for not crying to a man about some woman "ish."

As if things weren't already interesting, the morning we left Louisiana heading back to Georgia, Larry's ex, Damali, called. Larry put her on speakerphone so that I could hear their conversation. He knew about my trust issues from Marc and did whatever possible to gain my trust. She told him about a guy she met and was now dating. He was coming to Atlanta to see her. She said his name was John Anderson. I almost fell out. Larry's ex was dating my best friend's ex. Larry offered to take them to dinner so she could meet me as well.

Later that evening, we met John and Damali for dinner. It was awkward seeing John with someone other than Giselle. However, Larry calmed my nerves, and I felt well prepared for meeting Damali. When I first saw them, I greeted them as if they were old friends. But deep inside, it was awkward seeing a woman my Larry used to be in love with dating the man to whom my best friend used to be engaged. Life was so full of ironies. John seemed a bit on edge as if he was expecting me to bring up Giselle, but that would have been crass and disrespectful to all parties involved. As the night progressed, Larry and Damali went to the restroom, leaving John and me alone for the first time. We had time to exchange words, and I let him know I was staying neutral about his previous relationship with Giselle.

Before we went our separate ways, John thanked me for staying neutral and wished me all the happiness in the world. Damali hugged me and said she was overjoyed by Larry and me. She had such a profound authenticity about her that I hugged her back. Everything was so calm and perfect. Nonetheless, my phone's vibration brought a cloud to my sunshine.

"Hey, Gee!" I exclaimed as if everything was normal.

"I have been blowing your phone up...," she began, but I quickly interrupted.

"I know, we haven't too long finished dinner," I replied.

"So?" she insisted.

"John's doing well, and Damali is a nice person," I answered, trying to cut to the chase.

"And?" she hissed.

"And they seem happy." I replied, trying to think of what else she would like to know.

"Did he ask about me? Well, never mind. That would have been rude with her around," she both asked and replied.

"To be quite frank, John and I had time alone. So, to answer your question, no, he didn't mention you. I brought up the elephant in the room and basically told him your relationship had two sides, and I wish the best for both of you," I said, finally getting it out.

"What do you mean two sides? I am your best friend, and my side is the true side," she vented.

"Giselle, there are always three sides to every story, both persons, and the truth," I responded slightly annoyed.

"Wow, excuse me. So, I guess Damali will be your Maid of Honor also," she continued with both offense and sarcasm.

"If you don't want to be in my wedding, let me know, but last time I checked, you were my Maid of Honor," I said as my thermostat began to rise.

"I am sorry! I just don't know how to feel about all of this. I don't remember how she looks from that one time I ran into her at John's apartment. Do you think she's pretty?" she asked, changing topics like the weather.

"She's beautiful, both inside and out. You will eventually meet her," I said, forewarning her.

"I guess I need to prepare myself for that," she said in a low voice as if she was holding back tears.

"Giselle, I wish I could tell you that Damali was horrible and John seemed miserable without you, but that is just not the case."

"For Pete's sake, I see why Larry, John, and any man would love her. She is Damali. She's authentic, caring, smart, generous, and Christ-centered," I said, forgetting Larry was in the car with me.

"Wow, she sounds perfect! Well maybe he needs someone like Mother Teresa," she rebutted. "I don't walk on water, part the seas, or feed the hungry. I just try to be the best me I can be. If that's not good enough, then I don't know what is."

"Giselle, it is over! You and John are over! Damali did not break you two up! You need to get a grip! Sometimes, you really like seeing yourself as the victim! But in this instance, you're a woman who has a failed relationship. Join the damn club and keep it moving!" I finally unleashed the beast. Giselle has always had a tendency to be stuck on herself to a fault. I figured that was the main reason why her relationship with John failed twice.

"How dare you judge me in my vulnerability, Fatima! Just because someone finally fell in love with, you think you have the right to look down on others. I held your hand on more than one occasion while you were on a table...," she began spewing venom before I cut her off.

"Giselle, before you finish your sentence, we need to get off this phone. I know where the fuck I have been, the times your hands were there, and the times they weren't. I know who the fuck I was, I know who I am now, and who I want to be. And yes, finally I have a man who loves me. He knows the whos, whats, and whens and still chooses to love me, Fatima Antoinette Crosby! The unlikely candidate for a happy ending! I am not fucking judging anyone. I am living in my season and fuck you and anybody else who can't be happy for me! So, before this turns uglier than what it already is, goodbye!" I said, hanging up on her still hot from the moment but regretting my reaction and words.

I couldn't look at Larry. I was livid, and I wanted to call her back and tell her some things about herself. Nonetheless, no good would come from that. The hardest part of becoming the new creation that Christ says we can be is the motherfucking past. It is like thorns, nails, and sometimes a spear in the side. I don't have doubts about who I can be when looking forward, only when looking back. The reality of time is that no matter where you find yourself, you have an audience who always remembers your actions. I am convinced the devil takes permanent residence in our past, and God abides with us in the now. However, we are constantly making each moment the past. It is as real as yesterday. I am trying to make better decisions in my now so my yesterdays won't be painted with regret.

14 | Acceptance vs. Approval

"What's wrong, Fatima? It seems like something is bothering you," Larry inquired after midweek Bible Study.

"Just thinking about Maurice. The message tonight had me thinking about how things are between us," I said, trying not to feel guilty about what I heard.

"Was it the acceptance versus approval part?" he asked, reading my mind.

"Yes," I replied, putting my hands on my face. "Because I do not approve of Maurice's lifestyle, I no longer accepted him. But now, I feel guilty because God wants us to accept people although we don't approve of their behavior or sin. I was fine with how things are, and now I'm not. In addition to all of that, I feel bad for making him feel rejected especially now that my mother has shared with him that Mr. Peter is his father," I said, still trying to grasp the reality that Maurice was my half-brother.

"Well, what you are feeling is not guilt rather conviction. The Holy Spirit convicts us to change and to align our ways with God's ways. Someone can feel bad or guilty about something or someone and it has nothing to do with correction or God."

"Well, I feel convicted. What should I do?" I asked, wanting relief.

"Call him and have lunch or dinner with him when you get back," Larry said, putting the onus on me.

"Why do I have to call him? He can call me. Plus, he's barely talking to Mom," I rebuffed.

"Because the Holy Spirit didn't convict him," he said, kissing my forehead.

It was so awkward for me. I didn't know whether to call, text, or email Maurice. Unsure if he would respond, I texted him. I felt like my hormones were off since I started having irregular menstrual cycles. Hormones dictated in many ways how women interfaced with others. For some reason, I felt weird, and I was going to see my gynecologist to see what was going on with me.

Surprisingly, Maurice replied to my text message asking him to come to my house for dinner. I decided not to meet with him in public just in case things got turnt up. At that moment, I wished Larry and I lived together. Although I worked full-time in Atlanta, I got a short-term lease apartment until Larry and I wed and moved into our house. Larry thought it was best if we kept my brownstone in DC because it was paid off and the assessed value had tripled. I met with a management company that would lease my brownstone. Until it was rented, I would stay there when I came to town.

"Wow, I almost didn't recognize the place. You emptied it out. Are you keeping this furniture?" Maurice pointed to my living room and dining room furniture.

"No, they are staying here. Larry and I are getting new furniture, and my apartment in Atlanta is furnished."

"You live in an apartment?" he asked puzzled.

"Yes, Larry and I live separately. We won't live together until we get married," I said, dreading his response.

"Well, good for you," he replied nonchalantly.

"That's it?" I asked, shocked at his response.

"What am I supposed to say?" he asked, contorting his face.

"I don't know, but you normally have something sarcastic to say," I said regrettably.

"Well, when you're being a bitch, what else do you expect? I don't have a problem with you, Fatima, and now that I am your bastard brother, you probably really hate my guts," he said with piercing eyes.

"Well, since you mentioned it. I'm sorry," I mustered.

"What?" he exclaimed, almost choking on his food. "You're sorry? You didn't cheat on your husband and got pregnant with his best friend who just so happened to be married also," he said on a roll.

"But Maurice, she was broken," I interjected.

"Yes, and her broken ass cut all of us," he retorted. "She didn't love me. She kept my real father away from me to appease a son of a bitch that didn't love her weak ass."

"You used to defend her and now," I started.

"And now you do. That's fine because at least you know both of your parents," he said with tears in his eyes. "I hate her."

"No, you don't. You are very disappointed, and I get that, but you don't hate her," I said, trying to intervene.

"I hate you too, Fatima!" he said not flinching.

"I'm fine with that, and I deserve it. I haven't been a loving sister to you. I have been a total bitch, but Mom did everything for you. She has lived her life trying to give you everything to make up for you not having Mr. Peter in your life. She loves you Maurice, more than you know," I said, feeling sorrow from the depths of my soul for both my mother and Maurice.

"I know you are relieved that the skinny, gay boy isn't your brother," he cried, avoiding eye contact with me.

"I don't approve of how you choose to live your life, but I love you and accept who you are to me. You are my brother, Maurice," I said, getting it all out.

"You don't approve, but you accept. I don't understand what you just said," he stated with a quizzical brow.

"I have made some changes in my life, and number one is accepting Christ. In accepting Him, I realized that I was wrong for how I was treating you. Christ died not only for me but you too," I said, reaching for his hand.

"It took you accepting some white man with blue eyes and blonde hair that stars in Easter Sunday movies to accept your own flesh and blood family? If that's what it took, then I'm good," he said, trivializing what I said.

"Look, Jesus is more than some Hollywood persona. And yes, it is because of Him that I could accept you because prior to Him, I was broken and all I could do was cut people, including you. Maurice, I was living below my privilege of who He created me to be," I said with all sincerity.

"This is some deep shit. I would say you are using, but I know you don't get down like that," he said, shaking his head. "Well, just because Jesus gave you a new outlook on life, it doesn't change the things you have said or done."

"You're right; it doesn't. All I can do is say I am sorry and show you in my actions my heart of repentance," I said, smiling at him.

"I don't know how I feel about all this. No offense. My life is so fucked up right now. I still haven't met my father yet, and I hate my mother. To top all of that, my nightmare of a sister found Jesus and is engaged to the great White hope. It's a lot to take in. I need time to process all of this shit," he said, leaving me with no counter.

"I'm here for you, Maurice. Look at me. To be who God created me to be, the old Fatima has to die so the real one can strive," I said, hoping I wouldn't spook him.

"Are you feeling ok? You look a little ill, and you're sweating," he said, handing me a napkin.

"I'm okay. I just start sweating for no reason. Think I'm having hot flashes," I laughed.

"I heard you weren't getting any. Not getting dick will do that!" he exclaimed.

"I will marry Larry in a couple of months, and I am so happy, Maurice. Sex cannot compare to the feeling of satisfaction I have being with a man I can trust and who has my back," I said, beaming with joy.

"That's some deep ish. I don't know what to think. And they say you can't turn a hoe into a housewife," he jested but I didn't laugh.

"Maybe I was a hoe, but I'm not anymore. Maurice, I just wanted you to know that I love you and I am here for you whenever you need me," I said, maintaining my composure.

"Can I visit y'all in Atlanta?" he asked with a devilish grin.

"As long as you respect our home," I said in no uncertain terms, and he knew what I meant. "I would love for you to visit our church."

"Oh, hell nah. I don't want fire and brimstone to burn that bitch down when I enter the doors," he laughed.

"God loves you, Maurice," I said sincerely.

"He might, but the church doesn't," he said frankly.

"The church is His bride. We are a family," I said, hoping to make sense to him.

"Well, you know how sometimes in relationships you have the nice spouse and the mean one. Well, God is the nice one, and the church is the mean one. I'm good! Miss me with all those self-righteous, hypocritical Jesus-wanna-be's-but-will-never-be."

"If you died right now, where would you spend eternity," I asked as the opportunity presented itself. I did not invite him over to witness to him, but our pastor says when the opportunity presents itself, seize the moment.

"Hell, I guess. But, I'm fine with that, Fatima. No disrespect, I'm happy for you and Larry and your new life. I accept you, and hell, I approve too! You do you, Boo!" he said sternly.

"Did I offend you?" I asked, believing I went too far.

"I'm good. Just got a lot of shit going on. But for real, we're good," he said, when I noticed a tear in his eye.

"Maurice, I'm sorry if I offended you," I said remorsefully for whatever I did or said that made him sad again.

"Man, life is just so fucking crazy. I was going to hook up with this guy today, but I got your text message and decided not to go. Then right before I got here, one of my friends told me that dude has AIDS. That nasty ass bitch was going to give me AIDS."

My mouth dropped. I couldn't believe what I was hearing. It had to be the Holy Spirit that convicted and convinced me to reach out to Maurice. I hugged him tightly as we both wept.

"I'm so glad you answered me and came over," I said.

"Me, even more. I seem to be a magnet for misfortune," he said, shaking his head in despair.

"Maurice, that was my life six months ago," I said, remembering the darkness that shrouded my life. "But now, I am happier than what I thought I deserved."

"All because of a dude?" he inquired, looking puzzled.

"Yes, Jesus Christ. Larry was the vessel that made the introduction, but ultimately it was my decision to either accept or reject

Christ. Doing so has become the single, most important decision I have made in my life."

"I am amazed. Just listening to you, I'm like damn, who abducted my sister? I am happy for you; I hope it lasts. As for me on the other hand, I wish I could switch lives with someone else. My whole life has been a farce," he said with tears filling his eyes once again.

"Are you going to talk to Mr. Peter? Mom said he wanted to meet with you both. You said you felt like our dad never really loved you, and now here's the opportunity to perhaps experience that paternal love you longed for all your life," I said, trying to paint a brighter picture.

"Not our father, but your father. I guess I just need a second, and I don't know if I want her there," he said, still scorned by our mother's betrayal.

"You need someone there with you," I began.

"I agree wholeheartedly. You. Will you meet my father with me?" he asked.

"Are you sure?" I asked, shocked that he would even consider me given our tainted past.

"If Jesus has done all of this for you, then I need you to bring Him with you when I meet my real father," he said, smiling.

"I love to see you smile, Maurice. God knew about this, and He has a purpose for your pain. Trust me," I assured him.

"I wish He would have shown Himself to me earlier when I really need Him," he said in a despondent voice.

"Are we still discussing the same thing?" I asked, getting an eerie vibe from Maurice.

"Makes no difference. What I can say is I feel relieved knowing I was unloved because I didn't share DNA with Dad, I mean Craig Crosby," he said, taking a deep breath.

"Um, I'm confused," I said a little baffled by his statement.

"Before now, I believed I was unlovable," he said.

"Dad, I mean Craig, didn't know the meaning of love, and therefore, was incapable of demonstrating it. Nonetheless, we have each other and Mom, when you're ready to forgive her," I said, trying to end on a positive note.

"We'll see," he said. "I can't make any promises, but we'll see."

"Cool, just let me know when you're meeting Mr. Peter, and I will be there," I said, hugging Maurice.

15 | Engagement Party

Larry and I decided to get married in Atlanta despite his parents' discontentment about the wedding not being at their estate. Larry said whoever loved us would travel to us, which meant his family from Louisiana and mine from DC. Larry hired an awesome wedding planner for me who would create the wedding of our dreams.

We opted to have an engagement party instead of bachelor and bachelorette parties. This meant I would see my beloved in-laws again, and Giselle would formally meet Damali. I was not looking forward to their meeting. The only thing that could make this worse is if John came, but fortunately, he had a previous engagement.

"Love, are you ready for tonight? Are you and Giselle ok?" Larry asked once he arrived at my apartment.

"Yes, but you never know with Giselle. I swear she has multiple personality disorder. She's acting like the doting maid of honor, but who knows what she will be like when she meets Damali," I said with great uncertainty.

"Damali has a way of making people feel comfortable. I wouldn't worry if I were you," he said, kissing my forehead. "You're moist, babe. Are you hot?"

"I don't think so. Sometimes, I just sweat for no reason. I wake up in the middle of the night doused in sweat, almost like I peed on myself," I said a little embarrassed.

"Did you get your cycle yet?" he asked, knowing I had been skipping and missing.

"No, I'm dry. Very dry," I said, preparing him for my dried up holy coochie.

"I'm sure we won't have a problem," he winked at me. "Your GYN will let you know you are fine."

"I hope so," I said, trying to be optimistic.

"Mrs. Martin. I love the sound of that," he gleamed.

"So, does your mom, Lynn, and Melissa; they all are Mrs. Martin. I think I should hyphenate my name to add some pizzazz," I said, trying to get a rouse out of him.

"No problem. In my will, I will leave you 50 percent, adding a hyphen for pizzazz too," he laughed.

"Why? I'm 100 percent your wife!" I declared.

"Not if 50 percent of you is still in your father's name. The Bible says leave your parents and cleave to your spouse. That's 100 percent, not 50," he said in a serious tone.

"I was just joking, but now that you brought it up, marriage is 50-50," I shared.

"No Babe, divorce is 50-50. Marriage is 100. We are coming together to form one, and we are to give and share 100 percent of ourselves and resources with one another. When people divorce, what they have gets divided into halves," he said, making all the sense in the world.

"Well, I don't believe in divorce, so you're stuck with 100 percent of my crazy ass," I said, leaping into his arms.

"Is Maurice still going to make it?" he asked, knowing the truth behind Maurice's paternity.

"Yes, I still can't get over the fact that Mr. Peter is Maurice's father. However, when we met for lunch, I could see the similarities between them for the first time. They both can sing and have similar tastes in music," I said, recounting what turned out to be a harmonious reunion.

"Do you think Maurice will take Peter's advice about forgiving your mother?" he asked.

"I hope so. One thing I am certain of is that Mr. Peter never stopped loving my mother. Despite her concealing Maurice's paternity, he said he cannot and will not judge her. He was sorry for any pain or hardship he added to her life because of his lack of self-control and poor decision making," I said, thinking highly of Mr. Peter.

"Time, space, and self-reflection can mature a man. God wants us all to have His kind of love. Agape is unrelenting and never fails. The goal in marriage is to love each more in Agape rather than Phileo or Eros," he said, reminding me of sermons we experienced together.

"Would you have Agape love for me if I did what my mother did to my Dad or Mr. Peter?" I asked curious about his answer.

"I never would have married you knowing you loved another man," he said as a matter-of-fact.

"Well, let's say you did," I insisted.

"It's a hard concept because many of her actions were reactions. I can't imagine creating an environment where you didn't feel loved and appreciated," he insisted.

"Ok, this is all hypothetical. Entertain me," I pleaded.

"Is the real question what would it take for me to leave you? The answer is there is no answer. Can love conquer adultery, lies, and deceit? Unequivocally. Love conquers all. It's not the actual transgressions that end marriages but unforgiveness, bitterness, pride, and people's unwillingness to submit to Agape. When I marry you, Fatima Antionette, I am submitting to Christ so that I may love you without condition," he said, answering my question in a roundabout way.

"That sounds good," I laughed. "I guess we will see."

"We shall," he said, kissing me. "Woman, it's becoming harder and harder every day."

"I've noticed," I said, seeing his erection. "A sister is just glad her husband is packing."

"Oh, I'm packing alright and am going to unload all in you. You are the finest woman that ever walked this planet, I do declare," he said, shaking his head in total admiration.

"Lord Jesus, we're going to end up pregnant the first year," I said, shaking my head and imagining how our first time would be.

"Hmm, you think so? I was thinking the first month," he said, smiling and putting his hand on my stomach, "I can't wait to talk to our firstborn."

"I can't either; I know you are going to be an awesome father. You are wonderful with the children you mentor, and I am blessed that our children will get that love, attention, and direction every day of their lives."

"Well, I am glad that our children will have you as a mother, who will keep them grounded and connected to who they are. That is very important to me," he added.

"Well, they may have more of your hue and," I began.

"At the end of the day, our children will be Black, and they need to be proud of that and grow up in the richness of the Black culture," he replied.

"Well, why don't you just say how you really feel, Larry?" I joked. "They will be biracial, and their father is white."

"All of that is fine and dandy. We live in the United States of America and our children by race will be Black with a white father. Shoot, that's one of the reasons why we even have the Black race anyway," he said.

"Alright Massa," I joked.

"Don't do that," he said, not finding my joke funny.

"I was just joking. It happened to my people. It's all good," I said, trying to lighten the situation.

"It was horrific, and no, I don't joke about that. We can play about a lot of things, but that is not one," he said, kissing my forehead.

"Well, let's get ready to go. We have people waiting for us," I said, acquiescing.

Through my relationship with Larry, I have learned to pick and choose my battles wisely. What we learned through our premarital classes is that when you know a person's heart, debate is not necessary to prove a point at the risk of losing peace. The pastor also told us that some days we will have to choose between being right and having peace, and they will not always coexist in marriages. I was learning to choose peace, and that decision made my choices clearer and life appear less complicated.

When we arrived at our engagement party, it was breathtaking. The Martins insisted on paying for the engagement party and rented an entire restaurant that overlooked Atlanta. The place was filled with white roses, and candles and music filled the air. The first face I saw was Giselle's.

"Hello, honey. You look gorgeous," she said, hugging me tightly.

"Why thank you! You aren't looking too bad yourself," I replied, noticing she had all of her assets accentuated.

"Are we looking for a husband or are we sending a message?" I asked, cutting to the chase.

"John is past tense, and he's not coming anyway. I'm fine. Plus, I have something to tell you later," she said as if she was keeping a secret.

"Hey, Fatima darling," Mrs. Martin said as she hugged me. "You look grand!"

"Thank you, Mrs. Martin. You look beautiful as well," I responded when I felt a hand around my waist.

"Great taste just like your mother," my mother doted, kissing me on both cheeks.

I wanted to ask her if she was okay, but then another familiar face appeared, Mr. Peter. She told me he might come, and I told her I didn't mind as long as Maurice was fine with it.

"Hello Larry," Mr. Peter said, extending his hand. "I have heard nothing but wonderful things about you."

"I hope I live up to them," Larry smiled and hugged him. "We are huggers."

"I like him already, Fatima," Mr. Peter said, turning toward me unsure about whether to hug me.

"Everyone loves Larry. I'm thinking about piloting a television show," I laughed, extending my arms to accept his hug.

"Where's Maurice?" I asked, looking at them both.

"He's on the other side of the restaurant," my mother answered.

"Is everything ok?" I asked concerned whether they were getting along.

"Yes, don't worry. I have Peter with me. Enjoy your special night," she said, squeezing my hand.

"Fatima, how are you, hun?" Robert Jr., Larry's oldest brother, said as he hugged me.

"I'm doing well. Where is Lynn?" I asked, truly hoping she didn't make it.

"I think she went to the ladies' room with Melissa," he replied, signaling a waiter for another drink.

"Well, I'm glad everyone is having a good time," I said before Larry's mother grabbed my hand to introduce me to their extended family.

They traveled from Louisiana, Arkansas, and Mississippi. They were seemingly a nice group of people, some more taciturn than others. One common denominator was they were filthy rich. They owned oil fields to real estate in New York City. My family, on the other hand, was the epitome of the Black bourgeoisie. They were accomplished in most fields of achievement and believed in the empowerment and advancement of Blacks. The blending of our families was going to be a pièce de résistance of drip art. My family was from the upper echelon of Washington, DC, Chicago, and Houston.

As Larry and I made our rounds, I noticed Maurice was hitting it off with one of Larry's co-workers. For a fleeting moment, I wondered if he was gay. Whatever the case, I wasn't going to be concerned with his choices. I made a conscious decision to be a support system to him regardless of the direction he chose. I was happier that my mother and he could be in the same room at the same time.

"I would like to make a toast to my youngest son, Larry, and his beautiful fiancée, Fatima," Mr. Martin raised his glass.

"We ask God to bless your union with many children and years of happiness," he said, cheering.

I almost choked on his reference to many children. As I regained my composure, I noticed Lynn and Melissa smirking at me. I raised my glass to them and smiled. They irrated me, but luckily, I had so many other distractions, like Giselle.

"Fatima, I need to tell you something about Morgan," she started.

I hadn't heard her mention him since we found out he was engaged to a girl he rebounded to when Giselle rejected him for John.

"He's not getting married," she said with a weird look on her face.

"Ok, and what does that mean to you?" I inquired.

"Well," she paused as if something caught her attention.

When I turned around to see what arrested her, it was Damali, and John was holding her hand. I almost fainted, but Larry's arm was tight around my waist. We soon discovered his event was canceled, so he flew in that morning. The next shock was the gigantic diamond ring on Damali's finger. I was hoping that Giselle didn't see it, but no such luck.

"We've met," Giselle said, shaking her hand. "What a nice ring," she said, bringing everyone's attention to it.

"Thank you! We just became engaged over the past couple of weeks," Damali smiled and then looked at John who kissed her on the forehead.

"Well, I think congratulations are in order! This makes fiancée number two, John? If at first, you don't succeed, then propose again. I hope you make it to the altar," Giselle said with a facetious smile.

"Giselle!" I grabbed her and took her to the restroom.

"What the hell are you doing? This is my engagement party!"

"John wasn't supposed to be here, number one. And then, he has the nerve to propose to that bitch so when I saw her again, they could rub it in my face," she vented and abruptly stopped when she heard Damali's voice.

"You can write your narrative, but try using facts. John proposed to me on the anniversary of my mother's death. He knew that was a day I lamented and he wanted to replace that grief with joy, which he did," Damali said without pausing.

"I'm sorry," Giselle began.

"No, don't be. We can't always be the leading star; sometimes we must be the supporting cast. Today is about Fatima and Larry not John and Damali or Giselle for that matter. You and John shared love, but that season has long expired. He has moved on, and you must decide what you will do," she looked Giselle in the eye with such sincere purity, I dared not to say anything.

"Did you break us up or was it Kennedy? I need to know so I can have closure," Giselle vented.

"Neither. Nothing happened with Kennedy and him; she was an opportunistic primadonna. John and I haven't even had sex," she said, gently skipping the obvious answer, which was Giselle.

"So, it was me," Giselle said, bursting into tears.

Before I knew it, Damali was holding her. Tears filled my eyes, and I couldn't do anything except let them have their moment.

"I'm sorry, Fatima," Giselle said, regaining her composure.

"Don't worry about it. I'm just glad we can go on with our evening," I said when suddenly Larry burst into the restroom.

We all burst into laughter.

"Can I have my bride-to-be back?" He demanded unapologetically.

"So, you're just going to burst into the ladies' room," I jested.

"I will go to hell and back to get you," he said, grabbing my waist and kissing me.

At that moment, I felt a strong sensation like I was in the safest place in the world, in Larry's arms. As we enjoyed the rest of our engagement party, I looked at Larry from time to time and thought how blessed I was. We didn't have any drama, and we were on our way to living happily ever after. Who would have thought this could happen to me?

16 | POF

When someone tells you, they hope you rot in hell, I think of that as closure. However, Marc called me and told me he needed to see me; he needed closure. What the hell? I was getting married to Larry, and my life was on the up and up. Now, Marc, out of all people, wanted to bring drama about our sordid past. I asked Larry what I should do, and he suggested I meet Marc to see what he wanted. Larry said although we are free from sin, we don't get a free pass from the consequences. That perhaps there was some healing or forgiveness that was needed. I didn't wholeheartedly embrace what he said, but I was open to it.

The next time I flew to DC, I told Marc I would meet him for coffee. The day we met, I had an episodic climatic day that began with an early morning surprise visitor, Maurice. He appeared somewhat unnerved and disheveled.

"I'm sorry for stopping by unannounced. I didn't know where else to go," he said, walking right past me.

"What's wrong? Are you feeling well?" I asked nervously because he wouldn't stop pacing.

"I fucked up! Fatima, you gotta believe me, I've been trying to get this monkey off my back," he said, still pacing.

"Are you talking about drugs? I thought you said you only do weed," I inquired.

"I said the only illegal substance I have done is weed, but that's not the only drug I have tried or took," he said, looking ill like he hadn't eaten.

"What else have you taken, Maurice?" I asked apprehensive of his answer.

"Hydrocodone and Oxycodone," he said.

"Those are prescription drugs, Maurice. Where in the hell are you getting prescription drugs?" I asked.

"Being the son of doctors, it was easy when we were teens. However, as time went on, various friends had them or knew where to get them," he said, finally sitting down but shaking his legs.

"What are you on now and where did you get it?" I asked, hoping he would square up with me.

"I mixed Percocet and Vicodin," he said as he began nodding.

"Maurice, wake up," I panicked as I rushed to his side.

He started babbling incoherent words, so I called 911. While following the ambulance, I called my mother who said she would meet me at the hospital. Why is Maurice taking opioids was the question that kept racing in my mind. I knew finding out his paternity was a shocker; however, he was working his way through it better than I probably would have. He made a concerted effort to at least speak to our mother and was getting to know Mr. Peter. I couldn't shake the feeling that something else was haunting him.

"Hi Mom," I said, hugging her as she ran into the waiting room. "They are pumping his stomach."

"Oh my God!" she exclaimed in horror with tears in her eyes.

"Hey, sorry it took me so long. What's going on?" Mr. Peter asked as he joined us.

"They're performing a gastric lavage on him, Peter," she said, using medical terminology.

"What did he take?" he asked, looking at me.

"Percocet and Vicodin," I replied still unsure why.

"Do you know how much?"

"No, but he was pacing vigorously around my brownstone, and when he finally sat down, he passed out," I said, reliving that horrific moment.

"When did Maurice start using painkillers?" Mr. Peter asked my mother, who was still in shock.

"He was prescribed Hydrocodone when he was about sixteen, and that's because he got his wisdom teeth pulled. Outside of that, I don't know of any time he would have needed a painkiller and especially an opioid," she said, breaking down as if an ominous thought hit her.

"Honey, we are going to get through this together. Our son is going to be ok," he said as he hugged her.

"Fatima, do you know of any reason why your brother would want to kill himself?" Mr. Peter asked.

"Are you serious? You think he was trying to kill himself?" I asked in disbelief.

"We can't rule it out until we're able to speak to him," he said.

"It's ok, Baby. The doctors are going to ask us the same questions," my mother said, putting her hand on my leg.

"I knew Maurice was a recreational drug user and brought it to my mother's attention. I thought it was only weed, but he told me today he had been using opioids since we were teenagers," I said, feeling like a snitch.

"What? How?' my mother demanded.

"Evidently, he used to steal from you and Dad and forged your signatures," I said, no longer caring if I was snitching. I just needed my brother to recover.

"Oh, my God! Right under my nose! I failed you two horribly as a mother," she cried.

"Mom, look at me," I said, grabbing her face. "We may have failed you as children. What came first, the chicken or the egg? It doesn't matter because we all have scrambled eggs we need to work through so we can be whole," I said, trying to shift the focus off of her unto us all.

As surely as they predicted, the attending physicians asked us all the same questions Mr. Peter had. He concluded that Maurice needed to be kept for observation. His guess was Maurice accidently overdosed, but he was referring him to a psychiatrist. He was concerned that Maurice was facing deep problems and needed intervention. We all went to Maurice's room, and Larry asked that I call him and put him on speaker phone so that he could pray with us. His prayer was powerful and meaningful, leaving not a dry eye in the room. I gave Mr. Peter my number and told him to call me when Maurice came to. I knew my mother wasn't going to leave Maurice's side until he was able to leave the hospital.

Around noon, I made my way to the car still trying to wrap my head around what happened to Maurice. As I checked my phone, I saw missed calls and text messages from Marc. Although I wasn't in the mood to be around anyone, I wanted to honor my word and meet Marc.

"Hi, Fatima," Marc said as he stood to greet me.

"Hi, Marc," I said as I sat in the chair he pulled out for me.

"I was worried when I couldn't get a hold of you. Is everything ok?" he asked.

"I had a family emergency," I said, keeping it short and simple.

"Is everyone ok?" he continued.

"We'll see," I said, being curt.

"Do you need anything, I can," he began.

"What can I do for you?" I replied, cutting to the chase.

"I heard you're getting married," he said, looking at my ring.

"Yes, I am," I replied.

"Why?" he asked.

"Why am I getting married? Why am I marrying him? What are you asking?" I rebutted.

"I guess all of the above," he said, looking wounded.

"Am I missing something? Why do you care? Look, Marc, I agreed to meet you, but I'm not sharing my love life with you. We aren't exactly friends," I said, one step from walking out of the coffee shop.

"No, we're not friends. I guess we both are to blame for that. I don't hate you. I hate what you did, but not you. I love you," Marc uttered with a spark in his eye.

"What the f…?" I began, but he cut me off.

"I'm sorry for cheating on you. You didn't deserve that. You deserved more, but I was immature and insecure," he said, trying to touch my hand.

I moved my hand abruptly.

"I know it's probably too late for us, but I wanted you to know how I felt before you moved on into your new life with your husband," he said seemingly sincere.

"I think what happened between us was a necessary evil. In the aftermath, I had to do some soul-searching. Once I did, God brought Larry my way. Larry makes me want to be the best I can be. He makes me look forward to the future and all that it has to offer. I can't wait to marry him and build a family together," I said with tears welling in my eyes.

"Wow, I'm happy for you, I guess. That's a lot to digest," he said with a blank stare.

"I'm sorry for what I did and how I did it. That was inhumane. Please forgive me," I said, releasing tears that I didn't know I had.

"I forgive you. Please forgive me too," he said with tears in his eyes. "I wish I could have been that kind of guy. I always considered myself a nice guy, but that was always in comparison to scum-bucket friends."

"Everything worked out as it should," I said, wiping my tears. "All things work together for the good of those that love the Lord and are called according to His purpose."

"Wow, you seem so different," he remarked.

"I am, Marc. I made one of the best decisions that a human being can; I surrendered my life to Christ. The difference you see is Him."

"I never knew you to be a religious person," he said, looking amazed at the woman he saw before him.

"I'm not a religious person," I replied.

We talked for about an hour as I shared with him my testimony of how God changed my life. Many times, he looked at me as if he didn't know me. Sometimes, I barely recognized myself. I told him I would be remiss if I didn't share Christ with him because of what He did for my life. We prayed together before we went our separate ways. Larry told me that I had sowed an eternal seed into Marc's life and that mattered more than anything I had done previously. He said the things we do for Christ trump anything else we do. It felt good to do good. I felt like God breathed on me and had truly forgiven me for my sins, especially the abortions.

Everything was falling into place as it should. I loved my life. The sun was shining bright, and I was basking in it. From time to time, I thought this is too good to be true, and then it happened. My phone alarm reminded me of my late afternoon appointment with my gynecologist. I had a follow-up appointment to see what was going on with me. She had taken several tests and was going to share my results.

"Fatima, I did several tests to see why you are having infrequent menstrual cycles. Your ovaries are producing an extremely low amount of estrogen. What you are experiencing is called Premature Ovarian Failure," she said, arresting my heart.

"What is that? It doesn't sound good. Is there something I can do? Will it affect Larry and I getting pregnant?" I panicked.

"Basically, your ovaries are not functioning normally as they should for someone younger than 40. I can prescribe estrogen therapy for you. This can help with the hot flashes and osteoporosis, which are common with POF. Infertility can also occur as well."

"So, I'm going through menopause?" I asked completely scared and worried. My future was disappearing before me because of three words- Premature Ovarian Failure.

"Approximately one in every 1000 women between the ages of 15-29 and one in every 100 women between the ages of 30-39 are affected by premature ovarian failure or POF. POF and premature menopause are not the same. With premature menopause, women stop having periods before age 40 and cannot have babies. With POF, women can still have periods and in some cases, have babies," she said not relieving me.

"What about me? Will I be able to have children?" I needed to know because if not, I could not marry Larry. There was no need for him to suffer because of me. Having children meant a lot to him and his family.

"Your odds of conceiving are diminished; however, there are alternatives like in vitro fertilization."

"This is my fault, isn't it? It's because of the abortions." I cried. God was punishing me. I was forgiven, but not absolved from the consequences. I heard Larry's words resounding like a trumpet.

"Would you like me to explain it to your fiancé?" she asked.

"Oh, no! I'll tell him," I said, trying to hold back the tears.

"It's going to be ok. Knowing is half the battle. Don't jump to full-blown conclusions. Ultimately, God will have the final say-so."

At that moment, God seemed light-years away. My ovaries were failing, which meant my ability to procreate was failing, and ultimately, I would not be able to have Larry's babies. Having *childbearing hips* meant nothing without having functioning ovaries. I would never know what it feels like having a baby move inside of me or breastfeeding one. POF was inhumane; it reduced me to less than a human being. It made me feel like I wasn't a woman. The greatest thing to me that separated women from men was our ability to bear children. I was being robbed of that, and I wasn't going to allow that to happen to Larry.

17 | Catharsis

"Babe, you have barely spoken two words since you came back from DC," Larry said as he drove us to the final walk-through of the house we were buying.

"I'm just trying to," I began to say, but a lump got in my throat.

"Fatima, what is going on? You're scaring me," he said, pulling up to the house.

"We can't do this. I can't do this," I burst into tears.

"You don't want the house? Ok, we don't have to get the house," he said, looking bewildered.

"I can't marry you," I finally said.

"You can't marry me? Babe, are you ok? This is a joke, right?" he asked, looking completely puzzled.

"The doctor told me I have POF, and basically, I won't be able to have children. I know how much having a family means to you and your family. I'm defective," I said with tears cascading down my face.

"What is POF Fatima?" he asked, trying to touch my hand, but I declined his touch.

"It's Premature Ovarian Failure. It's when a woman's ovaries stop functioning under the age of 40. They can't produce eggs anymore. In rare cases, some can still have children with alternative methods," I said, regaining my composure.

"I know this is not the news any woman who wants to have children wants to hear, but Baby, you have to believe me when I say I don't care," he looked deeply into my eyes.

"Don't lie to me, Larry!" I yelled. "You love children, and you are great with them. Your family loves children too! I'm a Black woman with powdered eggs! What the fuck! This is embarrassing! God is punishing me for those damn abortions!" I said, getting out the car and walking away.

"Stop, Fatima! Where are you going?" he jumped out and grabbed me.

"Sex has its consequences, and the abortions have their consequences, which have been paid, but you won't bury them. You keep punishing yourself. Your biggest battle is in your mind. Christ forgave you, but at some point, you have to forgive yourself, Fatima," he said, holding me by both arms.

"I thought I had, and finally, I was going to have my damn happy ending. But I fooled myself, and I don't want you suffering because of me," I said completely heartbroken.

"Fatima, when storms come, we don't run and find shelter away from each other, we become the shelter we need together. What is a happy ending? Death? Because that is the only ending, and whether or not you're right with God will determine if it's happy or not," he said, drying the tears from my eyes.

"When I met you, I told you that the Bible says a man who finds a wife finds a good thing. You're my good thing, and you know why?"

"Why?"

"Because the rest of the verse says, he obtains favor from Lord. Fatima, since you have been in my life, God has blessed me. I am now the CIO for a Fortune 100. I am marrying the woman of my dreams, buying the house of our dreams, and serving God at our church through the men's and youth ministries. If God saw fit for us not to have children, I still couldn't stop thanking Him for what He has already done. If He never does another thing, He's already done more than what I deserve," he said with tears in his eyes.

I had never seen Larry cry, which made me cry even more. We held each other in the driveway of our new $3M home. How did I get here? How am I able to live beyond my past and find such happiness? Why do I deserve someone like Larry to love me?

"I love you, Larry, and Baby, I am trying to process your words, but it hurts so bad," I said, trying to fight the feelings of halfness.

"I feel like half a woman, and it's masticating my soul. Every time I see a pregnant woman or a mother with her child, their realities make me feel dead," I cried.

"Now, let the weak say I am strong. What you are going through might not be God-sent, but it can be God-used. He knew this day would come. He is your healer and the mender of your broken heart. He is the supplier of your needs. He is the lifter of your head. This challenge is not a surprise to Him; He's waiting for the champion in you to arise, Fatima. I fell in love with you because you are a fighter, and you go against the grain."

"I don't feel like fighting, Larry. I'm tired of fighting. I had to fight for happiness where some people just have it. Here," I pouted, giving him my engagement ring.

"Baby, don't! Don't do this. Don't be deceived by what others have. You don't know their stories, just like they don't know yours. I don't want to pressure or overwhelm you, so I am going to give you some time to think. If you still want to call off the wedding, then I will concede," he said, leaving me speechless.

What the hell did I do? Was I losing my mind? I couldn't eat or sleep. I took a week off from work. I wanted to be alone, away from people. The first two days, I couldn't get out of my bed. I couldn't muster the strength to reply to emails, texts, or calls. I had sunk into a bottomless pit; POF created hell for me on Earth.

GISELLE: *Fatima, I know ur busy, but pls return my calls. I really need ur advice.*

ME: *Wat up? I haven't been feeling well.*

GISELLE: *Oh, no! What's wrong?*

ME: *Just a little under the wedding?*

GISELLE: *Huh? Is there something wrong with you and Larry?!!!*

ME: *Sorry, autocorrect...weather not wedding. I'll call you once I take a shower.*

Man, I didn't want to tell Giselle about what was going on. I reminisced about conversations we shared, and little things slipped out that made me feel she thought she was better than me. At times, I even felt she was, but she was my best friend. I had to share my truth with someone, why not her?

"Fatima, I'm so sorry. Are you going to get a second opinion?" Giselle asked.

"No, I don't believe my gynecologist would make this up," I said, trying to remain calm.

"I know, but what does Larry say?" she questioned further.

"He's fine with us not having children," I said, holding back the tears.

"Wow, that's amazing. He loves you, Fatima," she replied.

"I know, and that's why I called off the wedding," I said, letting the tears flow.

"What! Oh, no! You found the love of a lifetime, and because of this one obstacle, you're willing to risk it all?" she insisted.

The nerve of her given that's exactly what she did with John.

"Now, I know this may sound hypocritical coming from me, but I learned a lasting lesson from my relationship with John," she continued.

"My glass is always half empty, and yours is always half full. Can you have babies, Giselle?," I said, cutting through her enlightened bullshit.

"Do I have a soul mate to create them with? " she said, shocking me with her quick wit.

"You did," I said, going beneath the belt.

"Touche. I'll let you have that, and yes, I had a man, an incredible man. However, he wasn't meant for me."

"Well, I guess Larry isn't meant for me," I replied.

"There is no perfect love story, sis. It's not whether the glass is half full or half empty. We should be happy to even have something in the glass in the first place," she ended.

"Touche," I replied before ending the call.

I guess there was some truth to what she said, but sometimes, feeling sorry for yourself feels better than the truth. The words I said to Larry replayed in my mind from when I judged John and Giselle's situation:

"I'm a babe in Lord, but I don't see letting anything get in the way of me marrying you!"

Then, I began to think about Larry and how he must have felt. He met what seemed to be the woman of his dreams, only to find out that he couldn't have it all with her. Then, she has the nerve to try to dump him because of her issues even though he is willing to overlook them. He is willing to take second prize. That line of reasoning made me feel sorry for both Larry and me. I wanted to call him, but every time I tried, I couldn't. Something had a hold on me. It was like a looming force, and every time I tried to look at the bright side, a dark cloud hovered.

Being in love has a way of making a person feel so damn vulnerable. Fatima didn't care about what people thought, but soon-to-be Mrs. Larry Martin cared very much. Married people represent not only themselves but also their other halves. Larry was on top of the world, and now he had an infertile, Black girl with childbearing hips from DC. I went to a top-tiered school, but some homecoming princess from a school I never heard of can pop out babies like popcorn. Larry didn't mind adopting, but I did. I wanted my children to look like Larry and me. I didn't want children who shared DNA with people we didn't know. We could adopt a genetically inclined murderer or rapist.

As my thoughts lured me deeper into the abyss of hopelessness, I heard a knock on my door. It was Maurice. What was he doing in Atlanta? Did he know? I almost didn't answer the door, but part of me worried if he was using again.

"Hey, sis," he said as he walked in looking better than before.

"Hey, Maurice. I didn't know you were in town," I said, opening my blinds and curtains.

"It looks like someone died in here," he said as he walked around.

"It feels like it," I said, not hiding behind pretenses.

"What's wrong? Is everything ok with you and Larry?" he asked.

"We're not getting married. I called it off. Maurice, I have POF, and there's a good chance I will not be able to get pregnant."

"I am not a gynecologist, and the last time I came near a vagina is when I was born; however, I didn't flunk English. You said there is a chance that you can't get pregnant. If there's a chance you can't, then there's also a chance you can."

"My doctor said I might have a chance with some assistance. Larry was like he didn't care. We could adopt for all he cares or have no children."

"So, let me get this straight; your doctor gave you options, and Larry gave you options. Fatima, what is going on here? I am confused. You are the judge and the jury and somehow don't want to give yourself options."

"I feel like half a woman, and it hurts. You can never know how I feel," I cried.

"I know what it's like to feel like a half woman. Fatima, I tried to kill myself," he said, leaving me befuddled.

"What are you talking about?" I asked bewildered.

"When I came to your home that morning, I had changed my mind and didn't want to die," he said, throwing me for a loop.

"You said it was accidental!" I exclaimed.

"I lied. I didn't want a suicide attempt being put on my medical record," he continued. "Sometimes, feeling half can make the whole you want to stop. Stop living, loving, trying, and so forth. It's a dark road, and in the middle of the darkness, I saw you," he began to cry.

"You convinced me with both your words and actions that Christ had not only saved you but also changed you. So, I came to you at my darkest hour," he said.

"Wow! I didn't even know you believed me when I said what happened in my life," I said, shocked by his words.

"I didn't want to believe you, but I saw a new person unfold before my eyes. It was surreal. In addition, you were there for me when I found out about Mr. Peter being my dad," he said with a serious look.

"It's the least I could do," I replied, reaching for his hand. "I love you, Maurice."

"Did you pray?" he asked, coming out of left field.

"What do you mean?" I replied dumbfounded.

"You said you gave your life to the Lord. Aren't Christians supposed to pray?" he asked, once again flooring me.

"Well, yes, but no I haven't prayed," I responded.

"Well, give me your hands," he said, grabbing them. "I don't know where to begin, but let's do this."

"God, I probably shouldn't be asking you for anything, but I am. I don't know if you hear me, but I am speaking to you not for myself but on Fatima's behalf. I know you know what's going and I am scared. I have never seen my sister like this. I am used to her being a lioness who roams the Earth fearlessly. But at this moment, God, she seems like a child who needs her father. Our father, well her father, wasn't shit and he isn't here, but she told me that you are our Heavenly Father. Well, I figure that has to mean something. We are your children; she is your child. Bring back her strength to fight. Although I just started going to church and this is all new to me, I was told that if I called on the name of Jesus, things could happen. Miracles could happen. Send us a miracle now in Jesus' name. Amen."

I couldn't get my nouns and verbs to conjugate. I couldn't believe what I heard. Maurice prayed for me and mentioned he was going to church.

"Wow, that was awesome!" I said, hugging him.

"I came here to fill you in on what's going on with me. After our acceptance/approval conversation, I felt like something was tugging at me. God spared my life, gave me the father I never had, and my sister, who I thought I hated. I thought I owed it to Him, to give Him a chance. In doing so, Fatima, I had to finally face my demons."

"What are you talking about?" I inquired, worried about his response.

Was Maurice about to tell me what caused him to start taking opioids?

"Fatima, I was molested by Mr. Porter," he said.

"Mr. Porter? Your 5th grade chorus teacher, Mr. Porter?" I said, becoming infuriated.

"Yes. One day when I was in the boys' bathroom, he came in there and put his hand on my shoulder. He said he wished I was his son and that I was gifted and special. He then began to touch my penis, and when I told him to stop, he said this is what all fathers and sons do. He showed me his dick and asked me to show mine to him. It felt so wrong, but I thought he wouldn't do anything to hurt me. So, I did, and he began touching it. Once it became hard, he made me touch his. He told me to put it away and not to tell anyone. When I went home, I was going to tell Mom, but she and Dad had just gotten into a big argument about him screwing his receptionist, so I kept it to myself. Slowly, he came up with "work" for me to do after school. That's when he started giving me head. He said I didn't have to suck him because he was the son and I was his father. He would moan and groan and tell me how good my dick was. Then he would masturbate in front of me. I remember one time his wife came to the school right after I came in his mouth, and he French-kissed her in front of me," Maurice recounted his story.

Hearing the violation that happened to him crashed down on me like a tsunami. I went from feeling self-pity and helplessness to wanting to find Mr. Porter and killing him. His daughter was my age and in my graduating class. Mr. Porter was voted Teacher of the Year, and all the students loved him. He was like a white Cliff Huxtable. I tried to talk

Maurice into pressing charges, but he said it was too much for him to deal with at the moment. I felt horrible for the way I had treated him growing up.

"I'm so sorry, Maurice, that this happened to you and I wasn't there for you. You needed someone, and I was too busy doing my thing," I lamented.

"Water under the bridge. I'm here in Atlanta because I have been connecting with a group of Black men who were sexually assaulted," he said.

"Huh? Are you serious? How did that happen?" I asked bewildered.

"At the engagement party, I hit it off with one of Larry's co-workers, and he told me about it?" he said as I looked in disbelief.

"So, I come down here a couple of times, but for the most part, I Skype into the meetings," Maurice said with a half-smile.

"So, does it help?" I asked.

"There are guys in there with worse stories than mine. Some were molested by their fathers, uncles, older siblings, mothers' friends, youth pastors, Boy Scout leaders, coaches, and more. However, the one thing we share in common is a feeling of brokenness," he said.

"Wow, that is so crazy," I said astonished.

"Sometimes, Fatima, it helps when you know you aren't the only person in the world that is shouldering a particular pain. By participating in this, it has helped me wean off drugs. Most days, I look into the mirror and like who I see. I picked up a little weight," he said, taking off his jacket.

"You look awesome, Maurice! Oh my God!" I exclaimed. Getting off drugs put about 10 pounds on him, and he looked awesome.

"So, what about you being…," I began to inquire.

"Gay? I'm trying to reconcile that. First, I am concentrating on being whole. My right to choose was taken away from me, and now I'm acting out of muscle memory, so to speak. But, I figure on my journey to wholeness, God will help me know who He created me to be," he said with tears.

We embraced each other and cried. I love my brother so much. He stayed the night with me, and we talked about everything from our sordid childhood to my POF crisis. While I spoke to Maurice, I began thinking what would Larry say? What would Larry do? I wanted to talk to Larry so badly. Since I've known him, he has been a constant refuge in times of trouble. He had a grander way of looking at things that brought understanding and peace to my chaos. My night ended with a text from Larry, which read, "I love you and miss you."

18 | Wholly

The next day, I lay in my bed all day reflecting on what Maurice shared with me, which made what I was going through seem diminutive. Through all these things, I felt like God was speaking to me. I wanted to go to the mid-week service but didn't want to run into Larry, so I streamed via my laptop. Our pastor was reading a scripture from the book of James, and it appeared on the monitors:

My brethren, count it all joy when you fall into various trials, 3knowing that the testing of your faith produces patience. 4But let patience have its perfect work, that you may be perfect and complete, lacking nothing. 5If any of you lacks wisdom, let him ask of God, who gives to all liberally and without reproach, and it will be given to him. 6But let him ask in faith, with no doubting, for he who doubts is like a wave of the sea driven and tossed by the wind. 7For let not that man suppose that he will receive anything from the Lord; 8he is a double-minded man, unstable in all his ways.

Then he shared The Message version of the same scripture:

2-4Consider it a sheer gift, friends when tests and challenges come at you from all sides. You know that under pressure, your faith-life is forced into the open and shows its true colors. So, don't try to get out of anything prematurely. Let it do its work, so you become mature and well-developed, not deficient in any way.

5-8If you don't know what you're doing, pray to the Father. He loves to help. You'll get his help, and won't be condescended to when you ask for it. Ask boldly, believingly, without a second thought. People who "worry their prayers" are like wind-whipped waves. Don't think you're going to get anything from the Master that way, adrift at sea, keeping all your options open.

I felt like a beaming spotlight was on me again! Was I doubled-minded? I was convicted. I was going around professing this new life I had in Christ, and when my first challenge came, I became like a wind-whipped wave. I didn't ask God anything, rather made indictments against Him by saying He was punishing me. I was under pressure, and my faith walk was whack as Hell. I was trying to get out of my marriage to Larry prematurely. I wasn't letting patience do its work.

I felt the Holy Spirit placing a salve on my soul. He reminded me of the service when I gave my life to Christ. I kept hearing the words Jehovah Rapha. Immediately, I searched for my download of that service so I could hear the words the pastor's wife spoke to me again.

"*Satan, you are a liar, and I rebuke you in the name of Jesus. Death, you have no victory, and you have no sting. Nothing will prevail against the blood of Jesus. Jehovah Rapha is healing right now. She will have double for her trouble in Jesus' name!*"

When she spoke those words to me, I didn't have a clue. I didn't know Jehovah Rapha meant the God who heals. Even if I did know, it wouldn't have made sense to me because I thought I was in perfect health. Was she speaking about the POF? Was death in reference to my ovaries? She said Jehovah Rapha is healing right now, but I wasn't diagnosed back then. For the first time since I had received my prognosis, I decided to talk to God. With a humble heart, eyes full of tears, and my hands lifted in complete surrender, I prayed.

"Father God, I don't know where to begin, but I will start with I am sorry. I am sorry that I talked to everyone else but you. I am sorry that I abandoned the gift of love you gave me through Larry because a challenge came my way. God, I am sorry for having faith like a damn wave. My biological father not loving Maurice and me created craters in our souls that we have searched high and low to fill. Lord, I now realize that those holes were never meant to be filled by anyone other than you. I am not worthy of your love, your forgiveness, or grace, yet you give it to me. I love you. Thank you for loving me at this moment, snot bubbles and all. You see me and through me and still love me. Lord, I want to be who you have created me to be. Let me love as you love and forgive as you forgive. I want to be whole, and that can only come from you. POF has to bow to the name of Jesus. If it is your will for me to have children or not, I consider myself so blessed to have all you have given me. Thank you for the healing happening in my brother. Lord, I hate what happened to him, but I am thankful that he is on his journey to become whole. Lord, thank you for Larry. I know I was tripping at first because of the wrapping the gift came in, but you are the ultimate gift-giver. Sometimes, I don't understand why he loves me as he does, but I know I have you to thank for that. Lord, teach me how to love, to truly love. Please mend whatever I broke with him. I want to marry him if he will still have me. Lord, please help me to see myself not as half a woman but whole. I want to see myself wholly as you do. In Jesus' name. Amen."

After that prayer, I felt like God breathed on me, and I had goose pimples all over my body. Immediately, I grabbed my phone and texted Larry, asking him to meet me at our favorite park. As I got dressed, I tried rehearsing what I would say and couldn't quite gather the words. Amazingly, I drove the speed limit; I didn't want a speeding ticket to mess up my date with destiny. Although I heard a voice saying Larry had changed his mind, I countered that voice with, "What God has joined together, let no man put asunder."

As I approached the park bench where Larry sat with his head in his hands, I felt a nervous energy. A voice said to me again, "turn around." Before, I could take a step further, he looked up at me. His eyes were red; he looked so thin like he hadn't eaten in months although we were apart for only a week. He stood instantly when he saw me.

"Do you want to sit or walk?" he asked.

"Let's walk," I said, trying to smile.

We walked for about five minutes without a word from either of us. The ball was in my court because I was the one who told him I couldn't marry him. I am the one who rejected him. I began speaking to myself, "I can do all things through Christ who strengthens me."

"Larry, so much has happened since we last saw each other," I said, trying to find the words.

"My childhood created areas of brokenness in me, and as I got older, my decisions only enlarged them. When I met you, things began to change for me. I never experienced the peace and love you presented me. However, the POF prognosis thwarted what I believed to be my fairytale."

He walked next to me silently, never once looking up.

"But, God came to me in various ways and showed me who I am. I am sorry, Larry, for putting you through all of this drama. I love you with my soul, and I want to be your wife. The possibility of not being able to have children with you devastated me. But, not having you in my life would be like death. You said it didn't matter to you, but I couldn't hear your words beyond my pain. Larry Martin, here I am with all of my perfect imperfections, letting you know that I want to spend the rest of my life with you if you will still have me," I said, crying from my soul.

Fear rose in me as I looked at him and he began to cry. He didn't touch me; he just looked at me with tears in his eyes.

"I don't know what to say," he began.

My heart began shredding. Larry didn't want to marry me any longer. He had time to think about it, and he decided he'd rather have someone who can procreate.

"I've had some time to think as well, Fatima. It's taken every ounce of energy I have to make it through each day. However, the more I thought about the situation, I began to see your viewpoint. I had to think deep inside, how important is it for me to have children? I had to be honest with myself. I also had to consider how you felt about it and the possible mental and emotional duress this will cause you for the rest of your life. I had to ask myself if I wanted to share the rest of my life with a woman who may never get over not being able to have children."

I tried to hold back the tears but to no avail. Larry was breaking up with me. I began to cry out to God, spirit to spirit. *Count it all joy* are the words that flooded my mind.

"I don't want to," he began, but I cut him off.

"It's ok, Larry. I don't blame you. I don't blame you for anything. I handled this poorly. I didn't even talk to God until last night," I said, but he interjected.

"Wait a minute, you prayed last night?" he inquired.

"Yes, but…" I started.

"I prayed too, and that's when I got the confirmation that I don't want to do life without you, Fatima. Getting beyond your walls was like World War 3, but once I made it over, I found an incredible soul. I feel alive when I'm with you. I would love to be a father, but I would rather be your husband. I told God last night, whatever His will is for us, whether children or none, I consider myself blessed," he said as he took me into his arms and hugged me tightly.

"Are you serious?" I asked as tears trailed my face.

"I love you so much. Please do me the honor of allowing me to be your husband. Life will not always be easy, but I believe all things will work together for our good. You are my good thing," he said, getting on his knee again and pulling the ring from his pocket.

"Yes, I love you and thank you for believeing in us and never giving up on me," I said as he put the ring on my finger.

Our reconciliation in the park remained in my mind from that day until our wedding. We closed on our house, which Larry insisted I live in instead of my apartment. It was 14,000 sq. ft. and would have been overwhelming to keep up, but Larry hired a maid and a groundskeeper, who were there every day. Larry would join me every night after work before he went to his apartment. During those moments, we would order furniture and go over our honeymoon details. We were going to the French Polynesia for two weeks. Sometimes, I had to pinch myself to make sure this "ish" was real.

My mother and Mrs. Martin worked on last minute wedding details with the wedding planner. Giselle was MIA for brief moments of time. I felt like something was going on with her, but I had a lot on my plate. I decided to wait until after my honeymoon to address it.

I received cards, gifts, and calls from so many people about our upcoming nuptials. I even received a text from Charles with a link from the Washington Post announcing our wedding. I dared not reply, and shortly after, changed my cellphone to an Atlanta number. Goodbye and good riddance to all the drama and those who brought it.

On our wedding day, I didn't have buttefflies, but I did hear the devil talking to me. It seemed like whenever I was doing what I believed God blessed and ordained, I could hear the devil's voice in Dolby Digital surround sound.

People are going to ask you throughout your lives why you didn't have children. Then, they're going to look at you and feel sorry for you. The white women who he probably should have married will say quietly among themselves, what a waste. Would you blame him if he stepped out on you and got someone pregnant? Could you blame him? One of those aborted babies could have been Larry's and your baby. Perhaps, even Larry Jr. Family means everything to the Martins. What the hell do you need that big house for when it will never echo a child's voice?

It became so unbearable that I began to cry. Giselle and my bridesmaid surrounded me and told me it was normal to have butterflies. They had no clue as to what torment painted the walls of my mind. Then, Mama pulled me away from them and gave me a pep talk. I focused on every syllable that proceeded out of her mouth.

"Fatima Antionette, greater is He who is on the inside of you than he that is in the world," she said, and for the first time, it made sense to me.

"And without faith, it is impossible to please God," Giselle said, putting her arms around me.

"Thanks, you two! I appreciate you. This, indeed, has been a journey, and I am glad you both were beacons of light when moments of darkness clouded my path," I said, hugging them.

Then, it happened; the ladies received their cue and departed. I was left alone with only God. Instantly, I felt like He hugged me and everything seemed good with the world. As I walked down the aisle, the audience was a blurred background. All I could see was Larry; he glistened like a sunray of love and hope. I felt guilty about the thoughts that flooded my mind minutes prior to me joining him at the altar. When our pastor got to our vows, Larry started first.

"Fatima Antionette Crosby, the honor I am asking you to bestow upon me is that of being my wife. From the first day I met you, I knew I could depend on you to be honest. Sometimes, that honesty hurt my feelings, although never intentional. Nonetheless, I was always able to see you. Sometimes, people spend their entire lives with someone and never truly know who that person is. I am blessed in that regard. When I think of my other half, it makes my heart smile. God gave me a gift in you. You are my good thing. Your allowing me to be your husband is an honor I will cherish, not take lightly, and will fulfill diligently. My full-time job is to be your husband. I put no career, person, or thing above you. I ask you to follow me as I follow Christ, and I know I can trust you to keep me grounded in this life God saw fit to bless us with. I vow to protect your heart, fuel your passion, feed your intellect, and love all of you until death do us part," Larry recited from memory.

"I do," I said with tears in my eyes.

"Today has been hard on me. Many of you might know, but Larry and I received news that my ovaries are failing and the chances of us having children are diminishing even as I speak. That news haunts me even now as I stand before you. So much, I called off the wedding a couple of weeks ago," people gasped loudly.

"However, we are here today, but by no virtue of my own. I never saw myself getting married, yet here I am. Never saw myself in an interracial relationship, yet here I am. Never saw myself going to church and growing in God, yet here I am. I don't believe I am anything outside of a miracle. It doesn't matter what you see concerning yourself if God sees something different. God showed His grace, mercy, and love to me despite my shortcomings and sins. Then, He gave me Larry."

"On the first day we met, Baby, you quoted the Bible where it states, "a man who finds a wife finds a good thing." When I called the wedding off, you told me the rest of that scripture: "and he obtains the favor of the Lord." God has blessed our lives beyond measure, and although I sometimes question the reality of our life together, God sends me gentle reminders in your words, smiles, and hugs. I don't know what our future holds, but I want to hold your hand as my husband until the day I die. Please do me the honor of allowing me to be your wife," I said, naked and humbled before all who witnessed.

"I do," he said.

"By the power invested in me by God and the State of Georgia, I now pronounce you husband and wife. You may kiss your bride," our pastor said.

Our wedding kiss lingered for moments. I could have stayed in his arms forever. Then our pastor announced us as Mr. and Mrs. Larry Martin. Everything seemed right in the world and the universe around us. As I looked at what appeared to be the endless faces of our guests, tears and smiles filled the room. The feeling of halfness that lingered over me after I was diagnosed with POF lifted and I felt whole, mind, body, and spirit. I can't recall a time when I felt freer than at that moment. Every so often when I glanced at Larry, he was already looking in my direction. Our spiritual connection felt supernal. As the day progressed, I anxiously awaited the moment when we would consummate our love and marriage.

19 | Us

"Happy Anniversary, Baby," Larry said as he nestled his face between my legs.

"Happy, happy," I said, barely able to speak the words.

"What, cat got your tongue?" he asked, as he continued licking and sucking.

"No, but evidently the cat has your tongue," I screamed in deep elation.

"Well, let's not disappoint her," he said as he slowly penetrated me.

He filled me completely, no holes or vacancies. Every stroke sent sensations from my nipples to my toes.

Making love was an excellent way to start our very special day. Many things happened over the past year with us, family, and friends. For beginners, I began volunteering at our church in the counseling ministry and realized that was my passion. A couple months into it, I decided I wasn't happy with my job. Larry encouraged me to quit and go back to school for counseling, which I did. I realized that I was at my best when I was helping others.

When I told Giselle, she was ecstatic. She felt like both of our glasses were running over. While I was engaged to Larry, she never quite got around to telling me about her new beau, Morgan. Morgan was her male best friend at some point, but while she was with John, Morgan confessed his feelings for her. It didn't end well, and Morgan got engaged to a single mother, who he told Giselle got on his nerves. The day of my wedding, Morgan was her guest. It was awkward seeing John, Giselle's ex-fiancé, with Damali, Larry's ex-girlfriend, and Giselle with Morgan, Giselle's former male best friend. However, it all worked out, and in a couple of months, Giselle became engaged to Morgan.

My mother and Mr. Peter started dating but then decided that they were better off as friends. However, Maurice enjoyed having the love of both of his parents, and it helped him kick his drug addiction. He moved to Atlanta and started volunteering in his church's recovery ministry. He also joined the church's choir and decided to break away from his singing group and work on his solo gospel album.

All was well with Larry; he was happy with his position and was frequently in the paper and on the news as a tech analyst. His face would still light up when he was around the youth ministry group and whenever he saw children in general. I brought up trying in vitro a couple of times and even adopting, but he said he believed God was able. Larry's faith made my faith stronger.

"Wow, what a way to start our anniversary," I said, kissing my gorgeous husband.

"Hoping to end it this way as well," he said, getting up and walking into the bathroom.

"What's next?" I asked curiously about what he had up his sleeves.

"We're going to breakfast," he said, turning on the shower. "Then, I have a couple of errands to run."

"Sounds good," I said, jumping out of bed and opening up the curtains to our two-bedroom bungalow suite that sat on the water with our own private plunge pool.

Larry and I flew in the day before to celebrate our anniversary in the French Polynesia where we celebrated our honeymoon, just at a different resort. The resort, like the former one, was breathtaking, and the service was impeccable. We had many dining options and activities to enjoy. To start our honeymoon, Larry arranged for dining on our terrace. In front of us was a beautifully hued lagoon and to our right was a green mountain range.

"When I look at His creation, I can't help but think about the Creator," Larry said, staring at me deeply.

"I know. This is beautiful and mysterious all at the same time," I replied smiling.

"Yes, you are," he said.

"I thought you were talking about all of this," I said, pointing to our paradise.

"It's about the same," he smiled.

"Why do you insist on making me blush?" I asked, taking in all of his adoration.

"I've gotta tend to a couple of things to prepare for tonight," he said, kissing me on the forehead.

While Larry was gone, I checked my emails, texts, and Facebook messages, which all flooded with happy anniversary sentiments. Little did I know, Larry posted a picture of us from our arrival at the resort on his fan page where he had a massive following. The caption read, *"One of the best decisions I have made in my adult life was marrying this woman a year ago tomorrow, second only to accepting Jesus Christ as my Lord and Savior. God is able. #MyGoodthing #TheMartins*

The post received over one million *likes* with the majority of them being *loves*. My husband was a celebrity in his own right, and no matter the platform, he always made mention of Jesus and me. There is a difference in knowing someone loves you and actually experiencing their love. Sometimes, people want to constantly live off of their past deeds and actions while taking a hiatus from refreshing their love through continued deeds and actions. This was a lesson that I had to mature at during the first year of our marriage.

One day, I asked Larry why he told me he loved me every day and sometimes multiple times a day, like when ending a phone conversation. I also asked why he found it necessary to compliment me on my appearance every day. He also had a habit of making a big deal out of everything I did. I began to question his sincerity. He told me yesterday's love would not get us through today's or tomorrow's troubles. Every day, I take the time to groom myself from head to toe, he said, and it should be complimented. Lastly, he said what is praised is also repeated. Whether an A on an exam or a delicious meal, he appreciates it and doesn't take even the smallest thing for granted. My life with Larry became my new normal, and it was hard to hold back when speaking to others, but I could share my true feelings with Giselle.

"Joyeux Anniversaire Madam," Giselle greeted me via videoconferencing.

"Mais oui, merci beaucoup mon amie. Est-tu bien?" I replied.

"That's all I've got. Girl, you know I had to Google that much," she laughed.

"Don't half step, if you're going to bring it, bring it, Baby," I jested.

"What are you lovebirds up to? I wasn't expecting you to respond to me for a couple of days," she said.

"Larry is running errands for tonight," I answered.

"I saw his post. Girl, that place is off the chart! Lord, I need to make more money. What are you two going to do tonight?" she inquired.

"I haven't the foggiest idea," I replied as I began wondering.

"Whatever it is, I know it will be supreme! That man L-O-V-E-S you, honey," she said.

"Speaking of love, what about you and Morgan? Have you two set a date?" I asked, still in disbelief that they were getting married.

"Yes, ma'am. We will be sending out Save-the-dates next week. However, as my matron-of-honor, I will let you know now. Our wedding date is this Valentine's Day!" she yelled.

"Wow! Ok, so you don't mind Valentine's slash Anniversary gift combos?" I said laughing, knowing I would.

"It's a sentimental day for Morgan. He said he's never shared a Valentine's Day with a woman he was in love with," she said.

"Well, I thought the only woman he has ever been in love with is you, and you two shared this past Valentine's Day together as fiancés," I said, feeling a little baffled.

"Bingo! Our second Valentine's Day will be as husband and wife," she said, putting her hands over her face.

"Are those tears of joy, Giselle?" I asked.

"Yes, friend. I never saw Morgan and me together. To be honest, I thought my world fell apart after John and I parted the second time. Running into Morgan at the same mall where Leslie told us they were engaged was a freak coincident. I didn't know he called off the engagement with her, and he didn't know John called off our engagement. We were two broken souls seeking solace in one another. When we finally made love, I felt like the healing process began for both of us. Although there were remnants of pain from our previous relationships, we loved each other enough to see through the issues and look at each other. I love him so much, Fatima, and he truly loves me too," she cried.

"Please don't take my previous conversations as me being against Morgan. I just want to make sure you're sure and that he is grounded in God. That is all. Relationships are hard enough and can be even harder when the two aren't reading out of the same playbook. You feel me?" I said, thinking about the times when Larry and I argued, and he would lead us in prayer.

"Every man isn't going to be a Larry, Fatima. You have an anomaly. Like you said, this is your new normal. The rest of us are trying to master just the normal," she replied.

"You aren't settling, are you?" I asked, needing to know.

"What I have with Morgan is better than what I thought I deserved. So, to answer your question, no. Enough about me, what about you? Did you find a gift for Larry?" she asked, redirecting my thoughts.

"It is immensely hard shopping for a man who has everything. If I see something I want for him, I generally just buy it. Luckily, before we left, I saw him ogling a tie on a website," I said, looking at the time. "Hey, I've got to get ready to go, he'll be back soon. I love you, Gee," I said, ending our videoconferencing.

When Larry returned, we took a snorkeling tour of the island where we saw exotic aquatic life. Next, we experienced a couple's massage after taking a coconut milk bath. After we got dressed for the evening, a boat took us to a private island where Larry arranged for us to have dinner. As we dined, our conversation morphed into forecasts of our next year of marriage.

"A year from now, I see us somewhere back in this region. However, you will be a certified counselor," Larry gleamed.

"Thank you, Baby. I couldn't have made it without your unwavering encouragement and support," I said, leaning forward to kiss him.

"I'm glad you're so close. You are missing something tonight," he said, reaching under the table and pulling out a white box with a simple white rose attached to it.

Inside was a beautiful statement necklace made of Tahitian pearls and diamonds. The baroque-shaped pearls varied in color with a dark green body color and peacock overtones.

"Amazing, Baby, this is so beautiful," I said, gasping for air. "This trip was enough, more than enough."

"Come on now. Don't play your boy like that," he said, doing the gangsta lean.

"Ok, tech guru by day and rapper by night," I jested.

"You're on to something. We might be cooking with bacon grease," he said beatboxing. "Maestro, hit it," he signaled to one of the servants who turned on a CD.

Only Larry, he thought of everything; the island, the food, the gift, and now the music. We danced and laughed for a couple of hours. Before we headed back to our bungalow, we walked hand-in-hand on the beach of the private island. When the moment was right, I took my gift out of my beach purse.

"Now, before you say anything, yes, I had to," I said, handing him the red foiled box.

"Wait a minute, I was just looking at this tie the other day," he said, shaking his head.

"Yes, something for your neck. Great minds think alike," I said, signaling for him to put it on.

"Wait a minute, there's something else in here," he said, slowly turning the applicator around.

"Oh my God," he said, falling to his knees. "Are you serious?"

"Yes, Baby, we are pregnant!" I said in total elation with tears filling my eyes.

"Babe, I don't know what to say," he said as he grabbed me around the waist and hugged me tightly.

"How far are you?" he asked still in total shock. "Wait a minute; you knew this when you went to your annual last week?"

"Baby, that's when I found out I am 10 weeks pregnant. You know with my periods being like they are and the POF diagnosis, I didn't think it was possible that I was pregnant," I said.

"Ten weeks? You don't look pregnant at all," he said as he began to weep. "God is good, and He is able," he leapt to his feet and grabbed me in his arms.

"There's more," I said, taking the paper that faced down in the box under the cotton.

"Is this the sonogram?" he asked, beaming with joy.

"Yep," I said, handing it to him.

"Am I reading this right?" he yelled. "Are those two babies?"

"Yes," I cried. "Yes, Baby, we are having twins! I didn't want to know the gender until you were with me. But, there you have it. Happy Anniversary, Larry! I love you so much," I cried as I hugged him.

When we made it back to our bungalow, we discussed the night I received Christ and our pastor's wife prophesying over me, rebuking death off my womb and saying God would give me double for my trouble. God turned my test into my testimony. When Larry and I returned home, we went to the doctor's office together to find out the sex of our twins.

That night as our celebration came to an end, I sat next to my husband, as he placed his hands on my stomach and began his nightly tradition of having a conversation with our son and daughter.

"A year ago, I married the woman that is carrying you. Your mother is the most amazing person who I am blessed to call my wife, and you are blessed to call your mother. I love you both, but so that we are clear, I love her more. She is living proof that the God we serve is able and will do more than our minds can even imagine or comprehend," he said, kissing my stomach.

When he kissed me, the babies moved. I felt the connectivity between us all. The word us had grown in meaning for me. I used to feel alone and singular, but when I married Larry, life shifted to us. As life settled, our oneness felt singular once again, but then God gave us Larry and Lauren, and we multiplied from two to four. I am so glad that a year ago, Larry and I didn't give up on us. Overwhelmingly, we both believe that if God doesn't do anything else for us, he's already done more than enough.